RECKONING AT DEAD APACHE SPRINGS

Other books by Kent Conwell:

RECKONING AT DEAD APACHE SPRINGS

•

Kent Conwell

AVALON BOOKS
NEW YORK

Published by Avalon Books,
an imprint of Thomas Bouregy & Co., Inc.
160 Madison Avenue, New York, NY 10016

Library of Congress Cataloging-in-Publication Data

Conwell, Kent.
  Reckoning at Dead Apache Springs / Kent Conwell.
      p.   cm.
  ISBN 978-0-8034-7600-4 (acid-free paper)
  I. Title.
  PS3553.O547R43 2011
  813'.54—dc22
                                                2011005606

PRINTED IN THE UNITED STATES OF AMERICA
ON ACID-FREE PAPER
BY RR DONNELLEY, BLOOMSBURG, PENNSYLVANIA

To my son, Todd, who achieved success where many fail.
He lives life as he chooses, enjoying it to the fullest.

Chapter One

 N o! Don't! I ain't never done nothing to you. I—"

An orange plume of fire lit the darkness, and the racketing explosion of a gunshot cut off the frightened plea. A dark figure screamed and tumbled back over the rump of his horse.

Lying on his belly beneath the thick branches of a wild azalea, Joe Phoebe held his breath as the scene unfolded less than twenty feet before him.

Half a dozen horses milled about, their riders only shadowy figures peering down at the writhing man on the ground.

"He ain't dead," one of the night riders muttered.

Another urged his pony forward. The starlight reflected off the silver conchos on the gunman's vest. He fired two more shots into the moaning shadow on the ground. "He is now," he laughed. "Clean out his pockets."

A second figure dismounted and rifled through the dead man's pockets. "Not much," he said, swinging back into the saddle.

As one, the band of gunmen wheeled their horses about and headed up the narrow road. Suddenly, one reined up and looked around. "What was that?"

The small band peered into the darkness surrounding the silent figure on the ground. One grunted. "There ain't nothing out there."

"Yeah," said another. "You're hearing things, Curly."

Joe lay motionless, daring not to breathe. He could feel the one called Curly staring at him.

After several moments, Curly clicked his tongue. "Reckon you're right. Let's go."

Joe remained motionless, stunned by the violence as well as his own close call. If those owlhoots had seen him, he'd be joining that other hombre stumbling down the Stairway to Hades.

The hoofbeats headed east, then cut back south. When the sound of pounding hooves faded, the lanky cowboy pushed to his feet and hurried to the prone figure. Odds were, the old boy was dead, but Joe had to be sure. He'd expect as much himself.

Kneeling, he laid his hand on the man's chest, then pressed his fingers against the vein in the man's neck. He shook his head. Death had branded this ranny for the eternal range.

Rising silently, he rushed back to his camp and saddled his roan. Seconds later, he was lighting a shuck west along the narrow road to Dead Apache Springs, where he was to meet up with his partner, Ira Croton.

He tried to push the murder out of his mind. He had his own set of problems without taking on any more.

* * *

A wad of tobacco in his jaw, Ira Croton studied his young partner. "A shooting, huh?"

A grin split Joe's weather-browned face. He paused before taking a drink of his morning coffee in the Red Hand Saloon. "Yep. I tell you, I was trying to dig a hole in the ground."

Ira, a rail-thin old Johnny Reb knocking on the door of fifty, leaned forward. He shifted his chaw to the other grizzled cheek. "How'd you happen to get yourself in that kinda predicament?" He grunted, and with a hint of wry sarcasm, added, "I knew I should never have let you go out all alone."

Joe snorted. "Don't hand me that malarkey. You'd have scooted down there faster than me. Their voices woke me up. I didn't know if it was a band of highbinders sneaking up on me or what. If it was, I wanted to surprise them, not the other way around."

The older cowboy shrugged. "I reckon I taught you good, after all."

With one hand, Joe made a flat, serpentine motion. "Anyway, I crawled around some boulders and dropped to my belly like a snake and snuck up through the underbrush. After they kilt the old boy, they headed back along the Waco road and then turned south. I'd seen a sign to a place called Abbottville. Maybe that's where they went. One of them was named Curly."

Shaking his head, Ira leaned back in his chair. "Well, I reckon we best just keep quiet about it, old hoss. I learned a long spell back never interfere with no one or nothing that ain't bothering me. Besides, we might have us a job hauling freight between here and Waco."

"Freight?"

"Yep." Ira drained the last of his coffee. "Our pockets is worn thin. We'll be moving about right considerable. It's a hundred miles or so to Waco. We'll meet a heap of folks along the way. Can't tell, one of them might recognize you." He paused. "You might find out who you really are."

"Don't lay no bets on it. I don't remember ever coming to Texas."

Ira snorted. "You're a Texas boy, no question. I reckon it's a mighty thin chance some jasper would know you, but you never can tell. Besides, we done drifted enough. Time to settle down."

A faint smile played over Joe's thin lips. "I won't argue you that." The younger cowpoke drew a deep breath. "Now, who's this gent we're going to work for?"

"Lemuel Mills. He's stove up in his legs, so his daughter takes care of a heap of the work. I reckon she's the real boss."

"A woman? In a man's business?" Joe arched a skeptical eyebrow.

"Don't get ahead of yourself. From what I've seen of the little lady, she knows dang well what she's doing." He paused and shrugged. "For as long as she can." The old Johnny Reb explained. "They got a big mortgage to meet. According to the old man, they're just keeping their heads above water." He pushed back from the table. "Let's go let you meet them."

Dead Apache Springs was a thriving village on the Leon River west of Waco. Some of the businesses lining the broad dirt street were of clapboard brought in from the east; others were of cedar logs; and like all pioneer towns, every third establishment was a saloon.

Catty-cornered across the street from the Red Hand Saloon sat Mills Freight and Livery. Adjoining the warehouse and barn was a corral that opened into a five-acre pasture in which a dozen heavy draft horses grazed.

Joe wrinkled his nose at the smell when he spotted several stacks of buffalo hides out behind the barn. "Hauling that too?"

"Yep. He pays an extra ten percent of what the hides bring to make up for the smell."

His dark eyes flashing in amusement, Joe replied, "For that kinda money, I'll haul them all day long."

They paused at the corral, leaning their arms on the rails and watching the back of a slight wrangler wearing a knee-length duster. The Stetson on the wrangler's head was crushed down over the jasper's ears, and he was wrestling mightily with a large black stallion that was doing its best to throw off the rope around its neck.

Every time the stallion reared on its hind legs, it would yank the cowpoke off the ground. Just about the time the bronc tamer seemed to have the upper hand, the horse pulled away once again.

"'Pears that old boy is a tad light for that animal." Joe called out good-naturedly, "Hey, partner. You need a hand with that cayuse?"

The wrangler glanced around just as the black mustang pawed the sky again. The cowpoke's hat bounced off, and a flood of brown hair fell down about the slight woman's shoulders.

Joe's eyes bulged. Ira shook his head and clucked his tongue.

Ellen Mills glared at Joe. A blush colored her cheeks. She was already irritated because of the headstrong stallion's stubbornness, and the fresh cowboy's remark set her off. She threw down the rope, and the black horse wheeled about, galloping to the far corner of the corral. In a waspish voice, she said, "You think you can do any better, cowboy, then have at it."

Ira whispered under his breath, "Now you done it, boy. That's the boss."

Joe groaned and laid his forehead on his arms, cursing his big mouth something fierce.

Striding over to the rails with her dark eyes flashing, the ruffled young woman snapped, "Well, you going to show me how it's done, or are you all bluster and horse feathers?"

The embarrassed young man raised his head. "Sorry, ma'am. I didn't—"

"Don't give me any excuses. Put up or shut up." She stood glaring at him, her fists punched into her hips.

Joe bit his tongue.

Ira grinned crookedly. "You heard the boss, partner."

Ears burning, Joe climbed through the rails.

Ellen climbed out and stood beside Ira. Taking the edge off her voice, she said, "That's your partner, huh? The one you told me about?"

Sliding his hat to the back of his head, Ira said, "That's him, Miss Ellen. He talks a little too much at times, but he's got a way with animals I never seen before. Just you watch."

As the two looked on, Joe eased across the corral toward the black horse, which watched the approaching human warily. The big animal laid its ears back, bunching its muscles to sprint away. Before it could, the man stopped and began talking to it.

When Joe stopped a few feet from the stallion, Ellen whispered, "What's he doing now?"

The old Johnny Reb scratched his gray hair and loosed a stream of tobacco juice onto the ground. "He's talking to the horse now. Calming him down."

"Talking? What's he saying?"

Ira chuckled. "The same thing you and me would say, but the way Joe there does it is something special. I've heard him. The words ain't nothing unusual, so I reckon it's something in his voice animals cotton to." He shook his head in wonder. "Like I said, it's real special."

By now, Joe had moved to stand under the stallion's head, gently running his hands over the trembling animal's arched neck. Slowly, he moved down to the horse's shoulders, gently massaging them while he continued to talk to the animal.

Disbelief filled her face. "I don't believe it. No one has been able to touch that black. Today was his last chance. I was going to sell him to the first greenhorn that came along just to get rid of him."

Ira's light blue eyes smiled in amusement. "Like I said, ol' Joe there, he's got a gift with animals."

Ellen crossed her arms over her chest. "Joe, huh? What's his last name?"

"Phoebe."

Her brows knit in puzzlement. "Phoebe? Like the woman's name?"

"Yes, ma'am." He paused and shifted his wad of tobacco to the other cheek. "You see, Joe there ain't got no memory of anything except the last couple years. The Army doctors called it amnesia."

"Army doctors?" Her face grew hard. "What side? I won't have no Yankee working for me."

Ira replied, "'Pears you got a big hate on toward them, ma'am."

She glanced toward the freight office. "You've seen my pa. A Yankee put him in that wheelchair when he went to bring my wounded brother home." She paused, her eyes growing cold. "Pa couldn't get to Virgil in time for doctoring to help. He died just after him and Pa got back. He's buried in the town cemetery." She looked back at Joe and the stallion.

Ira winced. "Sorry to hear that, Miss Ellen, but Joe there, well, no one knows which side he was on. The day Lee surrendered to Grant at Appomattox, a Federal patrol found Joe at Phoebe Pond, wearing nothing but red long johns held together by nothing but holes. That's where he got his name, Phoebe. We give him the name Joe too." Ira touched a gnarled finger to his head just above the temple. "A minié ball got him right there. He didn't know where he was or who he was." He drew a deep breath and released it slowly.

Before he could continue, Ellen shook her head. "Well, I'll be. I don't believe it."

Ira looked around. "I told you so."

Across the corral, Joe had slipped his finger in the bridle and was leading the cayuse, still somewhat skittish, toward the two of them. "Here he is, ma'am." A mischievous gleam glittered in his eyes. With a hint of challenge in his voice, he added, "Now what?"

Ellen heard the challenge. *Two can play that game,* she told herself. "Will he let you ride him? Or," she added, "are you afraid to try?"

Chapter Two

The Circle L Ranch encompassed over twenty square miles of lush valleys, rugged mountains, and tablelands of oak and cedar, all cut through by sweet water streams angling down to the Leon River, along which the ranch claimed a mile of shoreline on a sweeping bend to the northeast.

Inside the clapboard cabin that served as the chuck house, Henry Clay Brocius, foreman on the ranch, rolled his broad shoulders and raked half a dozen eggs onto his plate. The dim lantern light reflected off the conchos on his black leather vest. He was starving, having been too tired the night before to eat.

Slow-witted Herman Meyer, the Kraut, sat at the end of the table, slurping his coffee noisily from a saucer. Across the table, Navajo Dave eyed Brocius impassively. "What we got lined up today, boss?"

Brocius reached for the platter of fried venison. Without looking at the mixed-race Navajo, he said, "Reckon we wait to see what the boys found out last night."

9

With a grunt, Navajo Dave stabbed his slab of meat with the point of his sheath knife and tore off a chunk with his teeth.

Curling his thick lips in disgust, Brocius snarled, "You ain't got no manners at all, you know it?"

His black eyes glittering with amusement, Navajo Dave hooked his thumb at the Kraut, who was too busy shoveling grub down his gullet to pay attention to the conversation. "No worse than Kraut's," he replied.

Kraut looked up at the mention of his name, a confused expression on his round face. "Huh?"

Navajo Dave clucked his tongue. "We's just joshing around, Kraut. That's all."

Kraut knit his brows, not quite certain if Dave was making fun of him or not. One of these days, the bald-headed man told himself as he poked another massive bite down his throat, he'd show them just how important he really was.

At the end of the table, Brocius snorted and turned to his breakfast.

Navajo Dave tore off another piece of venison. "Wonder if anyone's run across ol' Andy yet."

The burly foreman cut his black eyes at Dave. His voice was cold and hard. "Don't you get to saying too much or you'll be a-joining him." He paused, his eyes boring into the wiry Navajo's.

The smile on the smaller man's face faded. Well aware of the mercurial temper of his boss, Navajo Dave grew somber. "Don't worry about me. I got nothing to say to no one."

Brocius glared at him coldly. Tension in the room grew palpable.

At that moment, Kid Pecos pushed through the door, breaking the growing tension. Dave sighed with relief.

Kid Pecos wore two hoglegs, tied down. He claimed each one had killed half a dozen hombres, not counting Mexicans or Indians. "Hi, boys. Well, I'm back. We can get started now," he said, glancing at the door as Curly Franklin, a quiet, cold-blooded killer who stopped counting his victims after the tenth one, entered. The expression on Franklin's face revealed nothing, like a blank sheet of paper with two cold eyes.

Kid Pecos poured some coffee and pulled out a bag of Bull Durham. While he rolled a cigarette, he reported to Brocius. "I did like you said. I counted close to three hundred head on Madden's south range."

Brocius winced. Three hundred. Twice what he expected, which was bad news. It appeared Madden was planning on staying, not selling out like Larson had figured.

Kid Pecos drew deeply on his cigarette and blew a stream of smoke into the air. "Just say the word, and me and Curly here could push them three hundred right up to Waco without no problem."

"You ain't pushing nothing nowhere, you hear?" He glared at Curly Franklin, whose expression had not changed. When neither gunslinger responded, Brocius looked back at the Kid. "You do what I say, when I say it. And nothing else. Understand?"

The slight gunman felt his ears burn. He toyed with the notion of calling Brocius out, but he had seen the big man's draw. While his own draw was a tad faster, the gunslinger had enough sense to know that even if he beat the larger gunfighter, he'd soak up a bucketful of lead himself. Besides, Brocius knew what he was talking about. "Sure. I understand. Whatever you say is fine with me."

Brocius turned back to his venison steak and eggs. "Good. Now belly up to the table. We're riding into Dead Apache Springs as soon as we finish. Larson wants us." Reaching for his coffee, he inadvertently struck the lip of his plate, turning it over and dumping steak and eggs onto his stomach and lap.

He leaped to his feet, cursing. His vest and shirt were covered with egg yolk and grease.

Navajo Dave snickered.

Brocius shot him a hard look. "Stop snorting like hogs. Get ready. I'll change and meet you in the barn."

Back in Dead Apache Springs, Joe Phoebe looked down at Ellen Mills, recognizing the challenge in her dark eyes and the taunt in the crooked smile on her lips. He glanced over his shoulder at the stallion. "Ride him?"

She lifted an eyebrow. "If you can," she retorted, inexplicably irritated he had so quickly gentled the stallion.

Ira watched the two closely, tickled at the interplay between them.

Joe stared at her for several seconds. Then, without a word, he turned and led the big stallion into the barn.

Ellen and the old Johnny Reb moved around the corral so they could watch Joe as he snubbed the jittery horse to a stall post. As he did, the office door opened, and an old man in a wheelchair pushed by a half-grown young boy rolled down the ramp into the barn.

The two, Lemuel Mills and his son, Colley, looked on while Joe saddled the animal, then walked it back into the corral. He paused several feet from the corral rails and called out to Ellen, "You're sure you want me to ride him?"

With a smug grin, Ellen came back with, "If you can." The taunting in her tone was unmistakable.

A faint smile played over his lips. He tugged his hat down tighter. "You're the boss."

Hooking his fingers in the leather headpiece, the weather-browned cowboy pulled the stallion's head back toward him as he swung lightly into the saddle. The horse bunched its muscles, but before it could explode, Joe tugged the surprised animal's head as far back toward the saddle as possible, then touched his heels to the horse's flanks, driving it forward into a circle.

The black stumbled and jittered about, then started moving in circles. After a short spell, Joe switched leads, pulling the animal in a tight circle back to the right, all the while tapping the confused horse's flanks lightly with his spurs.

After a few minutes, it widened the circles.

Ellen stared in amazement. She looked up at Ira, her eyes asking the question.

The old Johnny Red drawled, "I told you he had a way with animals, Miss Ellen." He paused and peered back into the corral. "And what's so all-fired curious about the whole situation is that he's got no idea how he learned all them things."

After several switches in leads, Joe called out, "Seen enough, Miss Ellen?"

Her eyes twinkled. "Reckon I have."

Joe eased the stallion closer to the rails, then reined

up. Loosening the reins, he leaned forward and patted the animal on the shoulder. "Fine horse here, Miss Ellen. Why, I . . ."

The big horse, feeling the pressure on the reins slacking off, grabbed the bit in his teeth, jerked forward, ducked his head down between his legs, and humped his back, sending the unprepared cowboy head over heels onto the ground. He raised a cloud of dust when he landed.

Ira and Ellen burst out laughing.

Joe sat motionless, embarrassed. He felt something at his shoulder and looked around to see the big black horse nuzzling at him. He reached back to scratch the animal's muzzle. "All right, fellow. I understand. I had my way with you, and now you had your way with me. We're even."

After Joe unsaddled the black stallion and rubbed him down, he joined Ira and the others in the freight office. Two windows overlooking the main street were open. A pot of coffee simmered on the potbellied stove.

Ellen introduced him to her father and brother. Gray-haired Lemuel Mills was in his early fifties, crippled when a Yankee patrol ran his buckboard off the road a few years earlier. Lemuel chuckled. "If you can handle four-ups and six-ups like you did that hoss, you got yourself a job for life right here, Joe." He paused, then added, "That is, as long as we can keep the bank from taking over the place."

Young Colley spoke up. "That was sure slick, the way you handled that stallion. Where'd you learn that? I'd have never thought of it."

Ellen offered Joe a cup of coffee. He nodded his thanks, then answered Colley's question. "I don't know. It just seemed kind of natural, you know, the thing to do. A horse can't buck if he's going in circles."

Colley frowned, so Joe explained. "I was in the war." He paused. "At least that's what Ira here says. Anyway, he said I caught a bullet in the head. Did something so that I got no memory of nothing before I woke up in a hospital two years back."

Colley, a slender youth nearing sixteen, looked at Ira. The old Johnny Reb added, "Him and me got us a job bullwhacking in Virginia."

Ellen grew somber. "What brought you here?"

Joe and Ira glanced at each other. Joe lowered his voice. "I guess you could say we're just sort of drifting."

"Tad more to it than that," Ira explained. "I been from the High Lonesome up in the Rockies to the shores of the Atlantic Ocean. I got me a ear for voices and such. I've heard them all. Joe here is from Texas." He paused, sipped his coffee, then continued. "We had to go someplace to find a job, so we figured, why not Texas? Who knows? Maybe one day someone will recognize him, or he'll spot something that jars a memory."

Lemuel Mills rubbed a bushy eyebrow. "Kinda thin hopes, ain't it?"

Joe replied wryly. "Life's kinda thin anyway, ain't it, Mr. Mills?"

The old man patted at his withered legs. "Reckon it is, Joe. Reckon it is. And call me Lem."

"Lem it is."

The pounding of hooves and the rattling of wagon wheels interrupted them. Colley glanced out the front window as a cloud of dust settled over the wide street. "It's

Mr. Needham, Pa. He stopped over to the sheriff's office, and looks like there's somebody laying in his buckboard."

Rolling over to the window, Lem squinted into the bright sunlight. "Why, you know, that looks like Andy Leland in the back, the foreman at S.T. Madden's Bar M." He waved toward the door. "Push me over there, Colley."

Ira and Joe exchanged anxious looks.

By the time the five of them reached the buckboard, a crowd had gathered, speculating in low voices as to who might have shot Andy Leland.

Sheriff Lewis inspected the bullet holes. "Where'd you find him, Hank?"

Hank Needham removed the straw he had been chewing on and used it to point up the east road. "About halfway between the Abbottville Cutoff and the Circle L Road."

Joe and Ira exchanged knowing looks. Andy Leland was the poor soul he had seen shot down in cold blood.

Chapter Three

Just before the cutoff. His horse was grazing nearby," Needham explained, slipping the straw back into his mouth.

Sheriff Lewis pursed his lips. He tugged his gun belt up under his overhanging belly and turned to his deputy. "Chester, ride out to the Bar M. Tell S.T. what happened. See what he wants to do with the body."

A neatly dressed businessman in a three-piece suit and a boiled shirt approached. "Trouble, Sheriff?"

Lewis glanced toward him. "Oh, Mr. Larson. It's Andy Leland. Hank found him out on the Waco road this side of the Abbottville Cutoff."

Larson stared at the body. "Robbery?"

"Don't know. Hank here run across him." The sheriff turned to search the dead man's pockets and grunted. "Empty, not even so much as his old Case knife."

Larson grimaced. "Looks like robbery to me. Still a bunch of them Northern scavengers roaming the country."

A chorus of agreement echoed from the crowd of on-lookers.

Three riders rode in from the east. Brocius rode up front, his rugged jaw covered with a week-old beard. They reined up at the buckboard. Brocius dipped his head to Hammond Larson. "Morning, Mr. Larson. Trouble?"

Joe looked up, taking in Brocius' steely eyes.

Larson gestured to the body. "It's Andy Leland. He's been killed. They found him out on the east road."

Brocius and his riders exchanged looks. Rolling his broad shoulders, the foreman grimaced. "Too bad. He was a good man."

Sheriff Lewis gestured to Hank Needham. "Take Andy over to the barbershop. Hymie'll take care of the body until we hear from S.T."

The small crowd broke apart.

From where he stood on the boardwalk, Hammond Larson watched as Ira and Joe accompanied Lem Mills to the freight office. He continued to stare at the closed door even after they shut it behind them.

Noting his boss' concentration on the strangers, Brocius rode closer. "Something bothering you, Mr. Larson?"

Larson pondered the question. "I don't know, Brocius. I don't know. Buy the boys a drink and come over to my office."

Inside the Millses' freight office, Lem turned his wheel-chair to face Ira and Joe. "How about it, boys. You want a job?"

Ira looked at Joe. "Up to you. I can throw my soogan anywheres."

Joe removed his wide-brimmed hat and ran his fingers through his short-cropped hair. "Why not?"

The older man smacked his hand down on the arm of his chair. "Good. We got us a couple regular contracts between here and Waco. We make a few other stops to pick or drop off supplies in the other small towns. Now that we got some help, we can hustle up some more work. Who knows," he added, "maybe we can even meet the bank note." He hooked his thumb at his daughter. "Ellen here will fill you in all you need to know. Pay's twenty-five a month with found, and Colley will show you where you can throw your warbags. We got a fair to middling spare room in the barn."

After tossing their warbags in their room, Joe and Ira were given a tour of the freight line, from tack room to feed shed. Pointing out two freight wagons, both Morgans, and a hide wagon parked behind the barn, Ellen explained, "We keep a spare wagon so we won't have any downtime. I'm sure you noticed that the roads around here are rougher than a cob. All that bouncing shakes the wagons up until they're ready to fall apart. Colley tightens one wagon up while I take out the load in the other one."

Joe looked around in surprise. "You?"

Ellen set her jaw. "And why not? I can drive as well or better than any man!"

Cheeks burning, Joe stammered, "I didn't mean that, Miss Ellen. It was just that I figured you . . . well, you know, a woman—uh—I mean, well, a man ought to be driving them," he added lamely.

"Maybe you're right, Joe, but out here, we do what we

have to do." She pointed out a canvas-covered stack of boxes on the loading dock at the back of the barn. "It's getting late. Load up those goods in one of the wagons. They're bound for the mercantile in Baineye Creek, about fifteen miles west of us." She paused. "Ira, you deliver them tomorrow. George Knowles is the store owner. He'll put you up for the night." She indicated a large, flatbed hide wagon. "While you're gone, we'll load up the wagon with flint hides. When you get back, you and Joe can run them up to Waco."

"Yes, ma'am."

"Flint hides? What's that?" Joe looked at her quizzically.

Ellen suppressed a smile, remembering what Ira had said about Joe's memory. "Dry buffalo hides. Wet, a hide weighs seventy-five to one hundred pounds. When they dry, they're hard as flint and only weigh about thirty pounds."

Joe eyed the flatbed wagon. Sturdily constructed, it was ten feet wide and almost three times that in length. The iron-rimmed wheels were fashioned from Osage orange wood and almost double the thickness of standard wheels on smaller wagons. "How many hides will it carry?"

Ellen cleared her throat. "We've carried two hundred before."

"How many do you have stacked up back of the barn?"

"Twice that many."

Joe whistled.

Ellen continued, "You'll pull out the day after Ira gets back. He'll follow in the Morgan wagon. Ira will be making stops in Abbottville, Valley Mills, and Carolina. There he'll pick up any express going to Waco. Sometimes we carry a wagonload. Sometimes, nothing but air. Still, we run the route twice a month." She paused, waiting for questions.

Joe shrugged. "Whatever you say, Miss Ellen."

Ira chimed in. "Yep."

In the saloon, Brocius ordered a round of drinks for his men, then, according to Larson's instructions, crossed the street to Larson's Mercantile, the largest dry goods and grocers west of Waco. From a spacious office in the rear of the store, Larson ran both his ranch, the Circle L, and the mercantile while continuing to build a network of influential politicians from Waco to Austin.

Hammond Larson was a large man, but his lofty ambitions by far dwarfed his physical attributes. He had learned the railroad would be coming through. With land, he could raise enough cattle to ship all around the country, bringing him all the wealth he could imagine. And with the wealth came power, enough power to move him into the governor's mansion in Austin.

When Brocius stepped into the mercantile, he spotted his boss, a cigar clenched between his teeth, standing at the window, observing Ellen and Colley Mills showing the two new cowboys around the barn and corrals. "Something wrong out there, Mr. Larson?"

Larson pulled the stogie from his lips. "Strangers. You ever see them?"

Brocius peered out the window. "Nope. Want me to find out who they are?"

Larson shook his head. "Let's wait. See what they do. They might ride on out."

"And if they don't?"

Larson looked around at his burly foreman in mock surprise. "Why, you might have to help them."

Brocius laughed. "Just say the word."

"Uh-oh," Larson grunted. "Looks like more strangers."

At the east end of town, three rugged hardcases rode in and pulled up in front of the Leon Saloon down the dusty street from the mercantile.

They hesitated before dismounting, studying the small town with wary eyes. One of them spoke and gestured to the sheriff's office.

"Recognize them?"

Brocius shook his head. "Saddle tramps! I don't like their looks."

The sun teetered on the horizon as Joe snugged down the last knot, stretching the canvas over the Baineye Creek shipment. He rose and stretched the kinks from his muscles.

Lem Mills wheeled himself out on the loading dock. "Ellen's got supper ready, boys. Wash up."

During a supper of beef stew and a dessert of sour cream coffee cake washed down with six-shooter coffee, Joe and Ira learned that Lem Mills and Henry Collins, the blacksmith, were the first two settlers of Dead Apache Springs. "Named it that because when we got here, there was a dead Apache up in the rocks above the spring, east of town. Henry found him. He'd been shot up pretty bad. Reckon he crawled up there to die."

"Saw it riding into town. Good water?" Joe asked.

Mills grunted. "Yep. Still has the coldest and sweetest water around here. Comes out of the rocks above. Someone said it was one of them artesian wells. I don't know about that, but even in the dry years, it keeps pumping water."

Colley spoke up. "How long ago was that, Pa?"

"Oh, about thirty years, I reckon. That's when we started building." The older man told how the small village had slowly grown, and how his business had expanded with it until the last year or so. "Used to get all of Hammond Larson's business from the mercantile, but he started hauling his own freight." He sipped his coffee and rolled a cigarette. "That's when we had to start running delivery routes." He shook his head. "It's been tough, but we've managed so far. Now things are looking up with you boys here."

Later, Joe and Ira ambled down the street to the Leon Saloon for a beer and a few hands of poker. They paused just inside the batwing doors, their eyes taking in the raucous shouts of the cowpokes about the room. Ira elbowed Joe, glancing at the three hardcases at the bar.

"I see them," muttered the younger cowpoke.

"They look like trouble, if you ask me," Ira grumbled, bellying up to the bar and ordering a beer.

With a snort, Joe said, "They probably said the same thing about us."

Across the room, loud voices broke out at one of the poker tables. His face ruddy and red from too much Old Overholt whiskey, Brocius raked in a large pot. Joe recognized him as one of the small group of cowboys gathered around the buckboard carrying Andy Leland that morning.

The three hardcases at the bar watched Brocius greedily.

One leaned toward another and whispered. The second ranny said nothing, just stared at the burly foreman.

Sometime later, Ira, claiming he was exhausted, went back to the barn. Joe remained, nursing his beer and watching the poker game. From time to time, he glanced at the three hardcases who kept staring at Brocius, who continued raking in pots. The hair on the back of his neck tingled. He had the nagging feeling of impending trouble.

Finally the burly foreman cashed in his winnings and pushed to his feet. He headed for the back door, and the three hardcases followed.

Joe paused, then hurried through the batwing doors. He had been right. There was trouble, and it was here right now in the six-guns of those three hardcases.

Chapter Four

The full moon was bright enough to read by. Moving as quietly as possible, Joe hurried down the shadowy passageway between the tonsorial parlor and the Leon Saloon. He paused at the corner. Not ten feet away, their backs to him, the three hardcases held Brocius at gunpoint, demanding his poker winnings.

Shucking his six-gun, Joe leaped from around the corner and slammed the muzzle of his Paterson Colt across one gunslick's temple, dropping him like a bag of corn seed.

"What the . . ." The second gunman spun at the commotion.

Joe grabbed the muzzle of the startled owlhoot's revolver and slapped him across the forehead with his own. In the meantime, Brocius jumped the third gunny and broke his jaw with a roundhouse right. The gunman collapsed.

Brocius kicked him in the ribs, and then started stomping at his head.

"He's had enough!" Joe shouted, grabbing the larger man by the arm and pulling him off. "Let's get away while we can." He ducked into the dark passageway and headed back to the street, where he turned back into the saloon.

Only a few heads turned their way when they burst in. Joe holstered his Paterson. "Come on. You look like you could use a drink."

Brocius grunted. "Reckon I could. I'm mighty glad you came along when you did." He stuck out his hand. "I'm Henry Clay Brocius. Everyone calls me by my last name."

Joe introduced himself and ordered two beers.

Brocius licked his lips after the first sip of beer. "I ain't fooling you, my mouth was getting mighty dry out there. I shoulda stomped that one into the ground. They'd of gut shot me and left me dying." He glared at the open doorway. "I might just do that if they show up in here."

Joe hooked his thumb at the sound of hoofbeats fading slowly to the east. "I don't reckon you'll have to worry about those old boys."

"Reckon not." Brocius grew serious. "You're a stranger hereabouts."

"Yep." Joe pulled out his Bull Durham and poured some tobacco. He offered it to Brocius.

The burly foreman grunted. "Thanks."

"Got in this morning," Joe said while twisting the ends of his own cigarette. "Me and my partner. Got a job at the freight office."

Touching a match to his cigarette, Brocius inhaled deeply, then blew a stream of smoke into the air. "Plan on settling hereabouts?"

Something in the larger man's voice nagged at Joe. He

shook his head. "A spell, I reckon. Then move on. Me and my partner, we got the wanderlust."

"The wander what?"

Joe replied, "Itchy foot. Just like to see new places."

Remembering that his boss had suggested Brocius might have to encourage the two strangers to leave town, he downed his beer. "Well, you ever get the urge to punch cattle, look me up. I'm the foreman out at the Circle L."

Later, Brocius assured Larson that the two strangers at Mills Freight were simply passing through. "They might hang around a few days, but they'll be moving on."

Ira pulled out well before sunup, fording the Leon just west of Dead Apache Springs.

Joe pulled the hide wagon in between two stacks of flint hides. By noon, he and Colley had stacked a hundred hides on the wagon. During noon dinner, which consisted of hot bread, warmed-over stew, and a small bowl of egg custard, he asked how many more hides Lem wanted them to load.

"A couple hundred hides ought to make a worthwhile load."

Two days later, Larson and Brocius stood looking through the front window of the mercantile as the hide wagon, followed by an empty freight wagon, pulled out for Waco.

Brocius cast a sidelong glance at his boss, wondering just what the Sam Hill was on his mind. Brocius was a simple man. He didn't understand men like Larson, who already owned more land than he could ever use yet still wanted more. He cut his eyes toward the barn and corrals of Mills Freight. It was a small operation, no threat at all to Larson, yet more than once Brocius had heard his boss express the desire to see the business fail.

He was firmly convinced that Larson wouldn't be satisfied if he owned half of Texas. Even Hammond's dream of the Texas governorship didn't surprise the gunman.

The weather held for the next week. Joe plodded along, struggling to make fifteen miles a day. Ira, stopping off at the various villages to pick up shipments bound for Waco and beyond, caught up with him at night.

Finally, they rolled into Waco.

After unloading the hides, they spread their soogans under the wagons, too tired to visit any of Waco's many saloons.

The second night, Joe and Ira enjoyed a beer at the Brazos Emporium. All of their business had been completed. Around his waist, Joe wore a money belt containing seven hundred dollars. Goods for delivery along the route had been loaded into the freight wagon, and they were ready to pull out next morning with the sun. "Here's to a safe trip back," Ira said, holding up his almost empty mug.

"A safe trip." Joe drained the last of his drink. "I reckon Lem is going to be mighty happy that we got such a good deal on the hides."

Ira chuckled. "I reckon he will."

As they turned to leave, a middle-aged range bum across the room pushed to his feet, dumping the hurdy-gurdy gal from his lap. His eyes bulged when he spotted Joe.

He hurried to the window just as Joe and Ira walked past outside. "I can't believe it!" he exclaimed. "He's still alive." He waved frantically for his sidekick.

"Yeah? What is it?" A half-drunk cowpoke slurred as he stumbled up to the window.

"I saw him. I saw Billy Reno."

The drunken cowboy stared at his partner. He shook his head and rubbed his eyes. "I didn't understand you, Red. What did you say?"

Red looked at his sidekick in frustration. "I told you, Charley. I saw Billy Reno. He's alive. I saw him riding out with Borke after the robbery. He's got to know where Borke hid the gold from the Abbottville Bank. With Borke dead, Billy's the only one who knows where the gold is." He spun on his heel. "Let's get him."

By the time the two drifters pushed through the bat-wing doors, the night had swallowed the man they called Billy Reno.

At the corner of the saloon, Joe and Ira cut down the narrow passage between it and the general mercantile next door. They crossed the dark alley and climbed through the rails of the corral where their horses were stabled. They had parked their wagons beyond the corral. Like the night before, they unrolled their soogans under the wagon bed and climbed between the blankets.

Back in the saloon, Red Coggins and Charley Lasater questioned the bartender who had served Ira and Joe. "Never seen them before," he said, wiping at the bar. "Reckon they're just strangers passing through."

* * *

By the time the sun rose over the oak and cedar table-land the next morning, the dust from Joe and Ira's departure had already settled.

Back in Waco, Red Coggins and Charley Lasater continued their search for Billy Reno. The two inquired at every saloon, livery, mercantile, and crib house, but no one recollected seeing the man.

After three days, the two hardcases were ready to give up until a chance meeting in the White Horse Saloon with two dusty teamsters washing out their dry throats. They had just hauled in two wagons of flint hides from the northwest, and were complaining that the previous load of high-priced hides had driven the price down fifty cents a hide. "That's a couple hundred dollars in any man's language," one greasy old skinner growled.

"Didn't linger about," said the second skinner. "Mort said they was only here two days. Left Wednesday morning before sunup."

Red cursed. "You get a look at them two?"

The first teamster loosed a brown stream of tobacco onto the sawdust floor. "Nah. They was gone afore we come in."

"This Mort. Who is he? Where can we find him?"

Leaning back in his chair, the teamster pointed out the door. "Why, Mort Brister down at the Waco Land and Cattle. Ever'body knows Mort."

Mort Brister was the everyman concept of a bookkeeper, short, slight, and garters on his sleeves to keep his stiff cuffs from gathering pencil lead. "Didn't pay a whole lot of mind. They was two of them. One young, the other older.

Maybe the young one's pa. Driving for a company called Mills Freight."

"You know where they went?"

He shook his head. "Never paid no attention." He paused thoughtfully. "They was in two wagons, one empty, the other loaded down."

That night in the saloon, Red Coggins had an idea. He pondered on it. He might be grasping at straws, but there was fifty thousand dollars in gold coins at stake. He wasn't about to give up until he tried every last idea to locate Billy Reno.

Chapter Five

Unlike the trip up to Waco, Joe laid over at each stop to help unload the goods. In Carolina, they dropped off bolts of cloth, a barrel of flour, kegs of black powder, and pigs of lead.

They delivered similar mercantile and farming goods in Valley Mills and Abbottville as well as both a ball peen and a four-pound blacksmith hammer to the Abbottville blacksmith.

Hammond Larson snipped off the end of a cigar and then touched a match to it. He took a long drag and blew out a bluish stream of smoke. "According to Lem Mills, those two hands of his are due in today. Don't forget what I told you."

"Don't worry," said Brocius. He had said nothing to his boss of Joe Phoebe coming to his aid when the three hardcases pulled their guns on him. Though deep down, the iron-fisted foreman had known better, he had hoped Joe and Ira would reach Waco and keep riding, saving him the trouble of forcing the two from town. Still, while he felt some obligation to Phoebe, that debt would not keep him from killing the younger man if necessary.

Larson continued to study the barn and corrals across the street. A faint sneer twisted one side of his lips. An idea had come to him. First thing after noon dinner, he'd drop by and pay a visit to Banker Phares.

To Larson's disappointment, the banker had taken the stage up to Fort Worth for a meeting with state bank regulators. "He'll be back in two weeks," the teller said. "Took the wife. Reckoned on a little vacation at Mineral Wells."

With a weary sigh, Joe pulled the wagon around back of the barn where Colley was waiting to help unharness the team. Ira rattled up behind in the Morgan wagon.

Ellen came out to greet them. "Any problems?"

Joe made a horizontal slice through the air with his hand. "Smooth as still water." He peeled off the money belt and handed it to her. "Here it is, eight hundred and twenty."

Her eyes grew wide. "Eight hundred and twenty, but—"

Ira explained. "We got three-fifty for the hides. Fifty cents more than we figured. Seems the demand is going up."

A broad smile wreathed her face. "Then we best not waste time getting the rest of these up there. But what about the rest of it?"

"Delivery fees for the goods we dropped off in Abbott-ville, Carolina, and Valley Mills."

* * *

After supper, Joe enjoyed a leisurely smoke and a third cup of coffee at the table while he and Ira answered Lem's questions about the trip, some for the fourth time.

"I figure if you want, we can load the hides tomorrow and pull out the next day for Waco," Joe said, turning up his cup and draining it.

Ellen nodded. "The sooner the better."

Ira rose and stretched his arms. "Fine supper, Miss Ellen. Reckon I'll hit the sack. Looks like my partner's got a big day lined up for us tomorrow. What about you, Joe?"

Joe reached for his hat. "Think I'll amble over to the Red Hand. Relax a bit."

A dozen or so cowboys milled about the saloon, half at poker tables, the other half leaning against the bar. In the middle of the room, a wagon wheel with four coal oil lanterns dangling from it hung from the ceiling.

Weary from the couple of weeks on the road, Joe bellied up to the bar and nudged his Stetson to the back of his head. He surveyed the saloon while waiting for his beer.

Brocius sat at one of the poker tables with four other cowhands. He had his back to Joe, who noted the burly foreman was wearing a black vest.

Looking over his shoulder, Brocius spotted Joe and waved the lanky cowpoke over to his table.

Joe paid for his beer and made his way through the tables. Other than the Millses, Brocius was the only person he had met in Dead Apache Springs.

"Howdy, Joe," bellowed Brocius as Joe came to stand across the table. His face flushed by whiskey, he added, "Boys, this here is Joe Phoebe. He pulled my bacon out of the fire a couple weeks back. You all best treat him right."

A chorus of amiable greetings came from the table, but Joe didn't hear them. The startled cowboy was staring in shock at the silver conchos on the black leather vest Brocius was wearing, just like the ones on the vest of the owlhoot who delivered the fatal shots to Andy Leland.

When he finally found his voice, all he could manage to say was, "Howdy, Brocius."

Pointing a meaty finger at an empty chair, Brocius said, "Have a seat. Join the game."

Navajo Dave joked, "Yeah. We need some fresh cash."

Joe shifted his weight from one foot to the other, his brain racing. "Thanks, but I ain't much of a poker player."

"That makes it even better," chortled Kid Pecos.

The whole table joined the hilarity.

Kraut stared blankly at the cowpokes about the table. Finally, he caught the joke and joined in the gaiety.

Joe indicated the vest Brocius wore. "Nice-looking vest."

Brocius touched a finger to one of the silver conchos. "Yep. Got it down across the border. Ain't none around like it."

"I reckon not." Joe sipped his beer, trying to still the pounding of his heart as he tried to figure out his next move. Finally, he said, "You just buy it? I didn't see you wearing it the other night."

Brocius concentrated on his cards. He shook his head. "Had it about five years now. It got spilt on. It was drying out."

The conversation lagged, and after several more minutes, Joe said his farewells and headed back to the freight barn.

Navajo Dave eyed Joe's back suspiciously. "You know

anything about that jasper, Brocius? I mean, other than he pulled your bacon out of the fire the other night?"

Shrugging his massive shoulders, Brocius grunted. "Nope. Just that Mr. Larson don't care for him to hang around here."

Kraut Meyer looked up, then focused his light blue Germanic eyes on Joe's retreating back. An idea began to fester in his mind. Maybe this was how he could show Curly, and even Navajo Dave and Kid Pecos, that he could do more than just run errands or watch the horses.

"That's exactly who he is," Joe told Ira, still trying to absorb the surprise of seeing the vest. "The old boy I helped out of that mess the night before we left for Waco. Henry Clay Brocius. You remember him. He was one of the riders who came up when we were all out there around the dead jasper, Leland. And he's the one I saw shoot Leland the night before."

Ira was sitting up in his bunk. He pursed his thin lips. "What are you going to do next?"

"I got no idea. Maybe the best thing is to talk it over with Lem. See what he might suggest."

Next morning behind the desk in his office, Lem Mills whistled softly and reached for his pipe. He said nothing while he tamped the tobacco in the blackened bowl. After touching a match to it, he said, "I ain't surprised. Brocius works for Hammond Larson. Nobody's yet to prove nothing, but seems like Larson has done mighty good for hisself in the five years he's been in Dead Apache Springs."

Joe and Ira exchanged puzzled looks. Ira thoughtfully

scratched at his bony jaw. "What do you mean by that, Lem?"

The older man grimaced. "Hard to say exactly. Nothing a feller can pin an idea on, but Larson is one of those fellers who always seems to have lady luck a-hanging on his shirttail. You know the kind. Nothing ever seems to go wrong." He paused and added, "That ain't the way life is from what I've seen," he said, laying his hand on one of his withered legs. "Things go wrong for everybody."

Leaning forward, Joe asked, "So, what do you think I ought to do? Go to the sheriff? Or is he in Larson's pocket?"

"No, not Jess," replied Lem. "He's honest as they come, though a mite slow to act sometimes." He ran his wrinkled and knotted fingers through his gray hair. "I reckon I'd say something to him, but he ain't the kind to jump into anything until he's figured it through and through."

Ellen pushed open the office door. "Breakfast is ready. Come on in and eat your fill. We got a big load to move today."

At the end of the street, east of town, two drifters pulled up into the rocks surrounding the spring of artesian water and let their ponies drink while they observed the slowly awakening town. "You reckon Billy's in this here town, Red?"

Tugging his floppy hat down over his eyes against the morning sun, Red Coggins slumped back in his saddle. "This is where the freight company he drives for is. Unless he's moved on, I reckon we'll find him here, but not under the handle Billy Reno. The kid's too smart for that."

"So, what do we do?"

Red sneered. "You wouldn't last a minute without me, you know that, Charley?"

"Reckon so, Red. I reckon so."

"I'll tell you what we're going to do. We're going to ride in, find the saloon nearest the freight office, then sit back and watch. Sooner or later, if he's in this here town, we'll spot him."

Charley shook his head. "Good idea, Red. Doggone good idea."

Red suppressed a smirk. He'd keep Charley around until he had the gold, then he'd send his old partner hopping over the coals in Hades.

Chapter Six

After a noon dinner of fried beefsteak, potatoes, and ice-cold tea, Ira and Joe threw themselves on the hay pile in the cool shade of the barn to relax from the morning's labor. They wanted to give the sturdy meal a chance to digest before readying the hide wagon for the trip over to Waco next morning.

While they were lazing about, Lem rolled out in his wheelchair. "Joe, need you to run a buckboard out to Norman Wilson's place. A couple boxes just got here on the stage that Norman paid us extra to deliver soon as they come in." He paused and scratched his head. "Don't know what they is, but they's heavy. Hitch up the sorrel. She's a good puller." He winked at Ira. "I figure old Ira here needs his rest more than you young whippersnappers."

All three laughed.

"Fine with me, Lem." Joe shot Ira a teasing look. "My partner is starting to get purty old and decrepit!"

"Decrepit!" Ira jumped to his feet and grabbed a bucket of water and hurled it at Joe, but by the time the water

39

splashed on the floor, the laughing cowboy was fifteen feet away.

Red Coggins had ambled out of the back of the saloon to the outhouse when Joe pulled out of the barn for the Wilson spread. Charley was busy at the buffet on the bar. Neither noticed Joe geehawing the buckboard out of town.

However, Joe's departure was not lost on Kraut Meyer. Ever since the night before at the poker table when Brocius remarked Larson wanted Phoebe out of town, the slow-witted owlhoot had dreamed about how he could drive Joe Phoebe from town, thus gaining the respect and admiration of his partners.

The Wilsons owned a small spread eight miles south of Dead Apache Springs. Joe had no trouble following Ellen's directions. Just after midafternoon, he rolled up to the small but neat cabin, behind which sat a log barn and two acres of corrals for stock.

The two boxes contained a harmonium, an organ operated by two large pedals at the bottom of the case to supply wind to the reeds. By the time Joe and Norman Wilson unloaded and assembled the harmonium, the sun was dropping behind the rugged hills to the west.

Wilson and his wife, Lela, insisted Joe stay for supper and an evening of joyous music on the new organ with which her husband had surprised her. "You can bunk up in the loft."

From atop a nearby crag, Kraut Meyer spent the night glaring murderously down on the Wilsons' cabin. And to make it worse, a sudden thunderstorm with heavy winds rolled in, drenching the disgusted German as well as the countryside and felling trees for ten miles around.

One of the pines fell right across the buckboard, splintering it in two.

The next morning, Joe looked down from astride the sorrel before riding out. "I'll pick up a wagon and come back tomorrow to salvage what we can of the buckboard."

Wilson waved. "We'll be here."

Up in the craggy hills overlooking the farm, Kraut Meyer swung into his saddle and raced back north through the forest to the spot he had selected from which he could fire down on Joe Phoebe. He figured that anyone hearing one or two shots would pay them little attention, chalking them up to hunters.

The first mile or so, Joe's sorrel tugged at the bit and crowhopped once or twice in an effort to shift the unaccustomed weight on its back.

Joe leaned forward and stroked her neck. "Easy, girl. Easy." The pony settled down and, after another mile or so, trotted along in a rhythmic walking two-step, occasionally grabbing at the bit or tossing her head.

The spot Kraut had selected overlooked the road where it made a long S, sweeping into a broad northward curve for a quarter mile, then east. From his position on a ledge twenty feet above the road, he had a head-on shot at anyone coming up the second curve.

His escape was just as well planned, he told himself. His gray gelding was tied five or six steps below, and once he killed Joe Phoebe, he could cut through the oak and cedar. Thirty minutes later, he'd be enjoying a cold beer at the Red Hand Saloon.

He waited patiently, his pig eyes staring at the road before him. The rain had softened the ground, deadening the click of hoofbeats. His quarry would give no warning before appearing around the bend in the road. So he wasn't too surprised when Joe Phoebe appeared, seemingly out of nowhere.

Kraut drew a deep breath to steady his nerves. He narrowed his eyes. Smiling grimly, he tugged the butt of the Henry Yellow Boy back into his shoulder and peered through the V-slotted sight just beyond the receiver. He lined the tip of the front sight blade with the top of the V on Joe Phoebe's chest and slowly squeezed.

The sorrel tossed her head once again, and a two-hundred grain slug powered by twenty-eight grains of black powder slammed into her muzzle, knocking her head around and sending her spinning to the ground.

Instinctively, Joe leaped from her back, hitting the ground and rolling into the underbrush on the side of the road. Jumping to his feet, he shucked his Colt. Without hesitation, he raced through the forest in the direction from which the shot had come.

Up in the rocks, Kraut cursed. He searched the forest, spotting among the cedars and oak a fleeting shadow that vanished as quickly as it appeared. Frightened, he scampered down from the ledge and leaped onto the back of his gray sorrel. He dug his spurs into the animal's flanks, sending it galloping pell-mell through a tangle of oak and cedar.

Hearing the crashing of underbrush, Joe angled off to his right, ignoring the limbs whipping his face. Through the thick growth of stunted oak, cedar, and large sweetgum, he glimpsed a gray horse, and then the forest swallowed it.

Returning to the dead sorrel, he pulled off the bridle and climbed up among the crags from where the shot had come. After a few minutes of searching he found a still warm rimfire shell, .44 caliber. "Well, well," he muttered. Whoever the backshooter was, he was using a Henry.

Climbing down from the ledge, he set out for town. All he had to go on was a gray horse and a Yellow Boy Henry. Such a combination shouldn't be hard to run down in Dead Apache Springs.

Upon reaching town, Kraut headed directly for the Red Hand Saloon. He planned on just one beer, then riding on out to the Circle L. He knew Brocius would demand to know where he'd been all night, but he'd simply explain that he had too much to drink and slept it off in the saloon's storeroom.

Just as Kraut was draining the last of his beer, Navajo Dave and Curly Franklin stomped in. Spotting the German at the bar, they bellied up beside him and ordered another drink.

Curly shook his head. "Brocius is fit to be tied. Where was you last night?"

An hour later, Joe Phoebe paused on the outskirts of Dead Apache Springs, studying the wide, muddy street before him and the two dozen horses hitched to the rails in front of the various business establishments.

His eyes narrowed when he spotted a gray horse in front of the Red Hand Saloon. Purposefully, he strode across the street and stopped beside the animal. His own clothes were soaked with his perspiration, clinging to his flesh like green bark.

Even if the horse had been lathered, there had been more than enough time for it to cool off. He ran his fingers under the saddle blanket, feeling the heat and sweat. His dark eyes studied the bridle, narrowing when he spotted the damp leather, the result of excessive sweating.

Reaching over the saddle, Joe pulled the saddlegun out of the boot, far enough to see that it was a Henry Yellow Boy. Grimly, he eyed the saloon.

Inside, he paused to accustom his eyes to the gloom. Several cowboys sat at tables dealing draw and stud poker. Another half dozen lounged along the bar.

With the empty shell in his hand, Joe crossed the room to the bar. He spoke to the bartender. "That gray outside. You know who he belongs to?"

At the end of the bar, Kraut had spotted Joe. He kept his pig eyes forward, staring into the mirror above the highboy.

The barkeep shook his head. "Nope." He called down the bar. "Hey, Dave. Any of your boys own a gray horse?"

"Yeah. Why?"

"This old boy was asking." The barkeep hooked his thumb at Joe.

Joe recognized the gunny as one of the men sitting at the poker table with Brocius. Then he saw the other two.

Brocius' boys also. In a soft, low voice, Joe said, "The gray horse yours?"

Navajo Dave narrowed his eyes. "Why?"

"Because if it is, I'm going to either kill you or make you wish you were dead!"

Chapter Seven

The room went silent, the tension palpable as a thick fog.

The Navajo stiffened, eyeing the cowboy facing him. The calm, almost peaceful expression on the young man's face unnerved the owlhoot. He swallowed hard and stepped away from the bar. He gestured to Kraut. "It belongs to him."

Kraut continued staring at the mirror.

Joe's cold voice cut like a knife. "You own the gray horse?"

Forcing his eyes around, Kraut sneered. "Yeah. Why?"

Joe slid the empty shell down the bar. "You left this behind when you tried to bushwhack me."

Kraut tried to bluff his way out. "You're crazy. I ain't been out of town all day."

Joe took a step forward. "You're either a liar or someone stole your horse."

Navajo Dave had moved a few steps aside. Behind Kraut, Curly Franklin moved away from the bar. Eyes glittering with amusement, both gunnies watched their partner, neither willing to come to his aid.

"I told you. I ain't been no place. My horse ain't moved none at all." Kraut licked his lips, and his small eyes darted about the room.

No one stirred. No one spoke. A deathly silence hung over the smoky room.

Joe eased away from the bar, his hand poised over the butt of his Paterson like an invitation. "Then I say you're a liar."

Kraut gulped. Sweat popped out on his round face. Fear showed in his blue eyes. He remained silent, motionless.

His voice cold as death, Joe growled, "You're not only a liar, you're yellow."

The Kraut stood frozen, his pig eyes darting about the room, pleading for someone to step in.

His face wreathed with disgust and anger, Joe glared at the big man. Before anyone could catch his breath, Joe took two steps forward and slammed his knotted fist into the bulky man's face, smashing his nose and splattering blood on bystanders.

Kraut flung out his arms as he stumbled backward, falling on his rump and turning a backward somersault on the floor. He sat up and grabbed his nose with both hands, howling in pain as blood coursed through his fingers, down his chest, and over his bulging belly.

Joe gestured for him to stand. "Get up, you back-shooting scum. You don't have the guts to face me with bullets, then stand up and take the beating you got coming, or I'll kill you anyway."

Sheriff Lewis pushed through the doors. "Hold on over there. Just back off, both of you."

A voice from the crowd shouted, "Kraut's on his tail, Sheriff! He can't back off."

The crowd laughed.

The sheriff ignored them. He stopped in front of Joe. "Now what's going on here?" He glanced back at the bloody figure of Kraut Meyer, then back at Joe. "Seems you've raised kind of a ruckus, cowboy. What's your name? What are you doing in Dead Apache Springs?"

Joe told him his name and explained he had gone to work for the Millses at the freight line. He glared at Kraut. "That one tried to bushwhack me this morning." He filled the sheriff in on the details.

After Joe finished, Sheriff Lewis pondered his explanation. "The gray horse and the Henry? That's all you got to go on, Mr. Phoebe?"

"Might not seem like much, Sheriff, but you know anyone else around that rides a gray and carries a Henry? A heap of folks still carry ball and caps, not rimfires. Like I said, his horse had been rode hard. You can't hide something like that."

By now, Kraut had staggered to his feet. With the sheriff in front of him and his two partners on either side, he grew belligerent. "You caught me by surprise, Phoebe. No one does that to me and gets away with it."

Joe took a step forward, but the sheriff's hand on his chest stopped him. "I did, and I'll do it again. You stay away from me. Next time I see you, I'll figure you're trying to put a lead plum in me. I'll put one in you first."

"Now that's enough, men." The sheriff turned to Curly. "You and Dave get Kraut back to the ranch. Keep him there. You hear?"

"I hear," said Curly.

After the three left, Sheriff Lewis looked back at Joe. "I ain't going to have no killings in my town, Phoebe. If there is going to be any justice served, it'll be at my hand, understand?"

Joe eyed the sheriff. "I won't start anything, Sheriff. You got my word. I like this town. The Millses are good folks. I wouldn't mind settling down in someplace like Dead Apache Springs." He paused, his eyes growing cold. "But any sidewinder that tries to backshoot me is going to find himself neck deep in an anthill."

Later, Lem Mills drew on his worn pipe thoughtfully. "You say you ain't never met Kraut before, huh?"

"That's right." Joe took a sip of water from the metal cup. "Saw him the other night at the poker table, you know, when I realized Brocius was the one who shot Andy Leland." He paused, then added, "Speaking of that, I should have said something to the sheriff this morning about Leland. I just forgot it in the excitement."

"Tell you what. Jess is an old bachelor. He takes supper with us from time to time. He looked up at Ellen. "We going to have enough supper for another mouth tonight?"

She laughed, like the gay tinkling of a glass bell. "We always have enough."

"All right. Call Colley in. He can take a wagon and reach Norman Wilson's place before dark. I'd just as soon he not be around when we talk to the sheriff about Henry Clay Brocius."

Out at the Circle L, Brocius glared at Kraut Meyer. "If you spent the night in the storeroom, how come Phoebe pointed you out as the backshooter?"

Curly and Navajo Dave looked on without expression as Kraut stammered. They knew the fat German was lying, and they knew why. They were as fearful of Brocius' fist as the Kraut.

"I told you. He made a mistake."

"A mistake. A gray horse and the Yellow Boy? Stop lying to me, Kraut, or I'll make what Phoebe did to you seem like a love tap."

Finally Kraut broke down and told the truth. "When you said at the poker table Mr. Larson don't care for him to hang around here, I figured I could help."

Brocius took a threatening step forward. Kraut cringed. The burly foreman shook his head. "You're so dumb you can't tell a skunk from a housecat. You know that? You kill someone, anyone, and it stirs up trouble. We don't want no more trouble. You understand?"

Kraut nodded.

"Good," said Brocius, and promptly coldcocked Kraut with a straight right to the chin. Massaging his knuckles, the burly foreman spoke to Curly. "When he wakes up, you boys got a job to do tonight. You know those three hundred head on the south range of the Bar M?"

Curly replied, "Yep."

"Scatter the herd. Run about a hundred head up north to Ghost Valley."

"You got it, boss."

Staring down at the unconscious gunny, Brocius reckoned he'd best have a talk with Joe Phoebe. He owed the young cowboy something for saving his life.

That night during supper, Joe related the night he witnessed Andy Leland's murder. "One of them was named

Curly. The other one, the one with the conchos on his vest, was Brocius. He was the one who killed Leland. And he said himself, that vest is the only one around."

The sheriff grunted. "That don't surprise me none. Curly would be Curly Franklin, one of Brocius' boys." He looked at Lem. "You know there's been a little trouble around here from time to time, stock running off or being stole. What I've noticed, and old S.T. Madden and me have talked about it, is that S.T. seems to be having a few more problems than other ranchers around here." He sipped his coffee and smacked his lips. "I got to say, Miss Ellen, you whip up the tastiest supper and best coffee I ever drunk. And I've drunk a heap." He looked back at Lem. "But Larson or none of his riders has done nothing against the law. Not around here. Not nothing I can hang my hat on."

Lem pulled idly at his bushy eyebrow. "What about Joe here seeing Brocius shoot Andy and hearing Curly Franklin's name? Don't that mean something, Jess?"

Sheriff Lewis grimaced. "Sure, it do, and I've no doubt you saw and heard what you said, Mr. Phoebe, but who can back your story up? All Brocius has to do is get his hands to swear he was somewhere else. You see what I mean? Even if your partner here saw it with you, I don't reckon we could get a jury in this town to convict him."

With a sigh, Lem sagged back in his chair. "Much as I hate to say it, Joe, Jess is right about that. Too many folk in town depend on Larson. I don't reckon we could get a jury."

Joe stared at the sheriff in frustration. "So now what?"

"Now all we can do is wait and watch, but if you want the truth, I—"

"It would help, Sheriff," Joe replied, unable to keep the frustration from his voice.

With a sheepish grin, Sheriff Lewis said, "The truth is, the only way we'll ever get Henry Clay Brocius out of our hair is when he gets gunned down. And he will, sooner or later."

In the Red Hand Saloon, Red Coggins and Charley Lasater huddled over a bottle of whiskey at a table in the rear of the room. Charley downed his drink. "If it be true that Billy has lost his memory, then what good does it do us about the gold?"

Red considered the question. "I been thinking on that. Could be that's just his story so he can start over somewhere away from the law. Or it might be on the up and up."

Cocking his head to one side, Charley asked, "So what do we do?"

Leaning forward, Red said, "Just this. Today when I was lazing about the freight barn, I heard talk about Billy and the old man he rides with pulling out tomorrow with a load of buffalo hides for Waco. You and me can just accidental-like drop in on them one night when they make camp. If Billy's just playing possum, we'll find out."

"What if he ain't?"

Red grimaced. "I heard say that sometimes when a person like that sees someone from his past, it sort of opens a door and they remember."

Charley poured another drink. "I sure hope he remembers." Pouring another drink, he added, "Be a blasted shame for that fifty thousand to just set out someplace where it can't never be found."

Chapter Eight

Early the next morning, Joe and Ira pulled out for Waco with the last of the flint hides. As they passed the bubbling spring for which the small village had been named, Ira glanced at the clear sky. "Another hot one, looks like."

Joe agreed. "I'll take the heat instead of rain, at least until we unload the hides."

The old Johnny Reb chuckled, running his gnarled fingers through his gray hair. "You're right about that. Them hides get soaked, this old wagon will fall apart."

They rode without speaking. The only sounds were the rattling of the wagon and the clinking of the chain traces in the O-rings and birds flitting through the forest of oak and hickory and cedar.

Midmorning they passed the narrow road cutting back to the southeast to the Circle L. Just before noon they approached the Abbottville Cutoff.

"What the—" Ira growled, sitting upright and peering at the lone rider in the shade of a giant sweet gum at the cutoff. Across the narrow road, a cone-shaped hill of layered black granite rose thirty feet into the air. "Hey, ain't that Henry Clay Brocius?"

Surprised to see the burly foreman on the road, Joe narrowed his eyes. He glanced down the Abbottville Cut-off, but the road was empty. Brocius appeared to be by himself. "Yeah. It blasted well is. Wonder what he's doing out here?" His brain raced. Had the killer learned of last night's visit with the sheriff? Was he here to assure there were no witnesses to the murder?

Echoing Joe's thoughts, Ira whispered, "Maybe he heard about last night." He scooted around on the bench seat and unobtrusively laid his hand on the butt of his revolver. "If he tries anything, he's a dead man."

A cigarette dangling from his lips, Brocius sat slumped in his saddle as the wagon drew near, his hands resting on the saddle horn. As they approached, he flipped the cigarette through the air and dipped his head. "Howdy, Joe."

With every muscle tense, Joe reined the team to a halt across the road from the smiling foreman. "Brocius."

Brocius cut his black eyes at Ira.

Joe introduced him. "He's my partner."

"I figured that. I've seen the two of you together. Mind if I ride along a spell?"

Joe leaned forward and wrapped the reins around the brake. If trouble came, he didn't want to be saddled with handling a team of frightened horses. "We was figuring on taking a short break for some grub. You're welcome to join us." His curiosity over Brocius' presence was growing.

Ira cut his eyes at Joe, surprised by the invitation.

Brocius shrugged. "Why not?"

Joe climbed down. "Why don't you pull out the grub, Ira? I'll tend the horses."

Ira headed for the rocks, but Brocius stopped him. "I wouldn't squat over there unless you want some rattlesnakes for company."

The lanky old man jerked to a halt. "Snakes?"

"Yep," the burly foreman drawled. "Don't know what it is about that place, but rattlers sure do like it. Hereabouts it's called Rattlesnake Hill. We best take our dinner under that sweet gum yonder. There's a log to squat on."

Joe looked at the five-acre patch of granite slabs. As he watched, two rattlers as big around as his arm slithered from a dark hole partially hidden behind a boulder and found a warm ledge on which to curl.

Squatting on a dead log in the shade of the sweet gum, Joe pulled out his bone-handled skinning knife and sliced off half a dozen slabs of fresh bread onto a square of oilcloth spread on the ground before them. Ira held out his hand. "Let me see the knife a minute." Unrolling a cold haunch of venison, he cut off a few slices and laid them on the oilcloth. He wiped the blade on his denims and laid it between him and Brocius on the dead log.

Eyeing the unusual weapon, Brocius folded a slice of bread over a couple of pieces of venison and took a bite. He hooked his thumb over his shoulder. "How many hides you carrying there?"

Ira remained silent. He didn't trust Henry Clay. He glanced at Joe. When the two of them looked around at the hides, Brocius slyly knocked the knife off the log.

"Around two hundred," Joe said. "Last of them. The Millses can use the money."

Drawing the back of his large hand over his lips, Brocius remarked, "I always reckoned Lem was doing right good."

"Was, but when your boss started hauling his own goods and supplies, it put a hurtin' on the business." He took a bite of his sandwich, and around a mouthful, said in a half-teasing voice, "Now, what is it you want, Brocius? You didn't ride out here by your lonesome just to take noon dinner with us."

Rolling his wide shoulders, Brocius fixed his black eyes on Joe's. "You know, I liked you right off. You did me a big favor. Usually, I don't take to folks, but I reckon I owe you a favor in return." He took another bite of his sandwich.

Joe and Ira exchanged puzzled looks. Apparently, Brocius knew nothing of the conversation with the sheriff the night before. Joe shook his head. "You don't owe me nothing for the other night. I was glad I could help."

Brocius swallowed. "Maybe so, but it'll make me feel like we're squared away."

"If it makes you feel better, fine."

Leaning forward and resting his forearms on his knees, the rock-jawed gunslick fixed his eyes on Joe. "Whcn you two hit Waco, keep on riding."

The simple words hit Joe between the eyes. "What?"

"Keep on riding. Don't come back to Dead Apache Springs."

Ira sputtered.

"We can't," Joe explained, his voice calm. "We've got Mills' money to return."

His hard face earnest, Brocius responded, "I'll go with you and bring the wagon and money back to Lem. You can trust me. He'll get every last penny the hides bring."

Ira burst out, "Ain't no one telling me what to do. Why—"

Filled with questions but no answers, Joe's brain raced to make sense of Brocius' request. He interrupted his partner. "We can't. You understand." It was not a question, but a simple statement. "Tell us why."

Tossing his unfinished sandwich to the ground, Brocius pushed to his feet. He shook his head. "I knew you wouldn't, but I had to try." He drew a deep breath and released it in resignation. "Well, I've done my best to do right by you." Moving slowly, he climbed into the saddle and looked down at Ira and Joe.

Joe stared back at the heavily muscled foreman. "At least tell me why you want us to keep riding."

"Because if you come back, I'll probably have to kill you." He paused. "I wouldn't want to do that, Joe. I like you. But if I have to, I'll kill you . . . and your partner."

Ira grabbed for his Colt. "What are you waiting for? Let's get the dance . . ."

Joe grabbed Ira's hand. "No." He looked up at the now scowling owlhoot who had not moved a muscle. "We'll be back, Brocius. I promise you that."

With a faint smile curling one side of his thin lips, he touched a finger to the brim of his Stetson. "I wish you wouldn't, but then, you been warned."

"He means it, Joe. He wasn't kidding none."

It was growing late. Joe was clicking his tongue as he turned the lead tandem into a grove of white oak and maple around a pool of water. "For the tenth time, Ira, I know he means it."

When he started to climb down, Ira exclaimed, "Hey, where's your knife?"

Joe grabbed at the empty sheath. "Blast. I must have lost it back at the cutoff. I cut the bread, and you sliced off the venison."

"I laid it on the log between me and Brocius. Maybe we rolled it up in the oilcloth."

The knife wasn't there. Joe shook his head in disgust. "Remind me to buy a new one in Waco."

"I still think we should have planted Brocius six feet under," Ira announced, unharnessing and picketing the horses.

"First things first," said Joe, building a fire and putting coffee on to boil. "We sell the hides first. Once back in Dead Apache Springs, we'll be able to get a handle on what's going on. One thing for sure."

Ira tossed their soogans under the wagon. "What's that?"

"Whatever reason is driving Brocius, it isn't too pressing, not yet. Otherwise, he wouldn't have bothered to warn us."

The thudding of hooves on the east road interrupted them. Ira shucked his six-gun and ducked behind the wagon. "It's Brocius. He circled around us."

Though skeptical the hoofbeats came from Brocius' horse, Joe disappeared into the shadows beyond the small fire.

The horses stopped, and from the darkness a voice called out the ubiquitous greeting from a stranger. "Hello, the fire."

Joe called out, "Come on in, slow."

Two riders materialized from the dark, hands held at shoulder height. "Just drifters, gents. Meaning no harm. Spotted the fire and thought we might share some grub."

Joe stepped into the light. "Step down, and welcome. I'm Joe Phoebe. This here is Ira Croton."

Red climbed down and faced Joe. "Name's Red Coggins." He paused, looking for some sort of recognition. When he saw none, he introduced Charley. "No offense intended, Joe, but you remind me of a young man I knew back before the war. His name was Billy Reno." The red-headed drifter studied Joe's face intently for any flicker of recognition.

Joe gave Ira a quizzical look that was not lost on Red. "Reckon I'm one of those jaspers with a plain-as-can-be face."

Red pulled out an oilcloth bundle from his saddlebags and sliced off several thick strips of bacon and put them on spits while Ira pulled out a flour sack holding several dozen corn dodgers, a staple of their diet throughout the two-week trip when they didn't feel like cooking.

After supper, the four sat around the fire smoking cigarettes and downing the last of the six-shooter coffee, so called because it was thick enough to float a six-shooter. Remembering the odd look Joe had given Ira when the name Billy Reno was mentioned, Red brought the conversation back around to Reno. "Yep, when I first saw you tonight, Joe, I woulda sworn I'd run across old Billy."

Instead of laughing and passing it off as he had done earlier, Joe leaned forward. "Who was this Billy Reno?"

Suppressing the excitement Joe's curiosity ignited, Red replied, "Just a sidekick way back."

"Around this neck of the woods?"

Red shook his head. "All around the state. We come through here once, back around '58 or so."

Joe glanced at Ira. He turned back to Red. "Tell me

about this Reno. Reason I'm asking is that in the war, according to Ira here, I caught a minié ball upside my head. I don't remember nothing before 1865. It's just one big blank. If I had a brother, you could be him and I wouldn't know."

A sense of disappointment washed over Red. "Must be tough," he remarked. In truth, he felt no sorrow for Joe, only for himself. It was frustrating, fifty thousand in gold coins, their location locked away in a mind that had gone blank.

Ira broke in. "Sometimes when I tell him about the war, one thing or another seems familiar, kinda jostles his memory, and he halfway remembers. We're hoping one of these days, he'll get all of his thoughts back."

A sudden idea had leaped into Red's brain. He pushed to his feet. "Well, we best be riding on. There's enough moon to see the road."

"You're welcome to roll out your soogans by the fire," Joe offered.

"No, thanks. We'll go on to Abbottville. We got business in the Abbottville Bank in the morning before we move on." He peered hard into Joe's face when he mentioned the bank, hoping but failing to see a flicker of recognition.

Joe just grinned. "Well, you take care, you hear?"

Chapter Nine

That night, Joe lay in his soogan, fingers laced behind his head, staring at the starry heavens overhead. Billy Reno! Somehow, somewhere deep in the murky recesses of his memory, the name had a familiar ring to it, but try as he might, every time he reached for a corner of the memory, it slipped from his fingers.

Midafternoon the next day, Joe noted that the narrow trace ahead of him had been torn by a multitude of hooves.

"Heap of beeves," observed Ira, shifting his chaw to his other cheek.

"Looks like." Joe scanned the trail that emerged from the south and continued northward into the wilds of the country. "Makes a body wonder what's back up there."

"It do that," drawled the old Johnny Reb.

They pulled into the hide yard in Waco just before dark a few days later. By noon the next day, the hides were unloaded, Joe had his new knife, and the two of them headed for the tonsorial parlor for a haircut, shave, bath, and new set of duds.

Later, standing at the bar in the Brazos Saloon, their conversation came around to Red Coggins and Charley Lasater. Ira said, "Who do you reckon that Billy Reno was?"

The rotund bartender paused in wiping the bar. "Reno!" He whistled. "Now there's a name I hadn't heard in years."

Joe looked at the shorter man. "You know him? Billy Reno?"

"Not him. Know the name, though." He shook his head, his shiny jowls flopping as he went back to wiping the bar. "Back in the late fifties, there was a gang of hardcases running around here and on up to Fort Worth, then down to San Antone. Word was that Billy Reno was one of them." He paused and looked up. "Like I said, I don't remember seeing him, but I did see his brother, Frank." He shivered. "Bad medicine, that one."

"Hey, barkeep. Two more beers here!" shouted a drunken cowboy down the bar.

When the bartender turned away, Joe, his brows knit in a frown, looked at Ira. The old Johnny Reb shook his head. "Nah, not a chance."

Joe drained his beer and set the mug back on the shiny bar. "Maybe not, but I'd like to hear more about this Reno jasper."

Reluctantly, Ira followed Joe outside.

Standing in front of the batwing doors, Joe looked up and down the dusty street and spotted the sheriff's office in the next block. Tugging his broad-brimmed hat down on his head, he said, "Let's see if he knows anything."

Ira laid his hand on his partner's arm. "Forget the sheriff, Joe. Let's have another beer. It's going to be a long, dry drive back to Dead Apache Springs."

"Come on. I won't take long. Like I said, I'm curious. Besides, I thought you wanted me to learn who I am."

Ira loosed a stream of tobacco onto the dusty street. "Reckon I do, but I don't want it to be nothing bad."

"Good or bad, a man needs to know the truth about himself."

The sheriff could only tell them the gang broke up eight or ten years earlier. He shook his craggy head. "Billy Reno was just a younker. Story was, he held their horses when they robbed the Abbottville Bank. Never could figure out what he was doing with them. He hadn't even started shaving. Rafe Borke, the leader, was shot, but he got away with fifty thousand in gold coins. They were never spent, never found. Best guess is he hid them, then died from the gunshot wounds. Found him just outside of Valley Mills."

Ira pursed his lips. "You remember any of the gang's handles?"

The sheriff grimaced. "Been quite a spell. They didn't bother us up here too much, just the smaller towns. There was one named something like Call . . . McCall . . . that was it. Then there was a Bill . . . Donovan, if I ain't mistook. They was kilt at the bank. There was one or two more counting the Reno youngster."

The old Johnny Reb eyed Joe knowingly, then he turned to the sheriff. "Any of them called Red or Charley?"

Pondering the question, the sheriff began to shake his head slowly, then paused. "Seems like there was a Red . . . Red . . . something."

Joe started to supply the name, Coggins, but Ira knit his brows and gave an almost imperceptible shake of his head. He explained after they left the office that the sheriff might have begun to wonder where they came up with the name and start putting two and two together.

"Two and two together." He paused. "You think I might be this Billy Reno?"

"No, no, I don't mean that. But on the other hand, partner, ten years back, you was just a younker, wet behind the ears. Probably like most young'uns, so dumb you couldn't hit the rear of a cow with a banjo."

Joe chewed on his lip. He didn't cotton to the idea that he might have once been an outlaw, a bank robber. "Maybe so, but I ain't no owlhoot."

Ira laid his gnarled hand on his partner's shoulder. "No, you ain't, son. You sure ain't."

Two hours out of Waco, the rain struck, a slow, steady drizzle at first, then it became heavier. For four days, they bounced on the wagon seat, hats tugged down over their necks, and their backs hunched against the rain.

During the nights, they hung a fly that kept the rain off them while they boiled coffee and fried bacon and smoked cigarettes, but the ground was too muddy to roll out their soogans, so they spread them on the wagon bed and pulled a canvas over them for shelter from the rain during the night.

* * *

By the time they caught sight of Dead Apache Springs, they had worn out the pros and cons of Billy Reno like a linsey-woolsey shirt stonewashed one too many times at the creek.

They rolled into the small town that sat drenched and soggy, the ruts in the street filled with water. From behind the batwings of the Red Hand Saloon, Henry Clay Brocius narrowed his eyes and cursed when he saw the two cowpokes pull into the freight line corral.

As Ira reined the team to a halt, he said, "Brocius was watching us from the saloon."

"Yeah, I know." Joe kept his eyes forward.

"What do you reckon he's going to do now?"

"Got no idea, but whatever it is, he'll make it look like he had nothing to do with it."

Ellen came out of the office into the barn and greeted them. "How'd it go? Prices still up?"

Ira grimaced. "Not quite. Three bucks a hide, but still, you got six hundred here." He looked past her into the office. "Where's Lem?"

"Pa'll be back directly. Banker Phares called him over there for something—I guess about the bank note."

Glancing over his shoulder in the direction of the bank, Joe said, "That's funny. I went over there with Lem when he deposited the last hide money. He made a couple payments ahead."

Ellen turned back to the office. "Well, we'll know soon enough. Come on in after you take care of the horses."

The three of them were sitting around Ellen's desk drinking coffee and discussing the trip when the door slammed open and Lem, his heavily wrinkled face red with anger, rolled in, spouting vehement curses.

"Pa!" Ellen shouted. "What's wrong?"

The older man stammered with fury. He jabbed a finger in the direction of the bank. "I'll tell you what's wrong. That weak-spined banker sold my note to Hammond Larson, and that no-account, snake-headed sidewinder is calling it in."

The young woman stared in disbelief at her father. She pressed her fists to her lips in shock. "But—he can't do that."

Lem nodded. "Yes, he can."

"But how? That doesn't seem fair."

"There's a clause in the agreement saying the bank can call in the note with sixty-day notice. It's always been there, and up until now it's always been nothing more than a formality. But that lowdown scoundrel has done took advantage of it."

Ira cleared his throat. "How much do you owe, Lem?"

The older man grimaced. "Too much. Almost four thousand. Ain't no way I can raise that in two months."

Ira's eyes flashed with anger. He laid his hand on the butt of his Colt and looked at Joe, his eyes asking the question.

"No." Joe shook his head. "Guns aren't the answer."

"Then what is?" Ira demanded.

"I don't know, but guns will just get us more trouble. We need to sit down and talk it over nice and calm."

Ellen glared at him. "How can you talk about calm? My father's about to lose the business he's worked all his life to build."

"I know. I also know if we put our heads together, maybe we can find an answer. Jumping up and charging across the street with guns drawn won't solve anything." He paused, then added, "Besides, it could be this is just one part of a bigger plan."

Lem cleared his throat. "Huh? What do you mean by that?"

Joe leaned back in his chair. "Remember when you said that good things seemed to happen to Larson and bad things to everyone else?"

Running his fingers through his gray hair, Lem said, "Yep."

Ira leaned forward. "What are you driving at, hoss?"

"That maybe, just maybe, Hammond Larson is one of those greedy scalawags who wants everything he sees, and he doesn't want anyone to interfere."

"I don't follow you," said Ira.

Joe continued, "There's a heap of folks out there like that. Don't kid yourself. That would explain why Henry Clay Brocius said he might have to kill us if we didn't leave town."

Ellen's eyes grew wide. Lem caught his breath. "He what?"

"That's right." He filled them in on the meeting with Brocius at the Abbottville Cutoff. "For some reason, he, and I figure he's talking about Larson, he wants Ira and me out of town, and if he has to, he'll kill us."

"That's right," Ira said. "I was all ready to start the dance then, but Joe here, he stopped me."

Ellen frowned. "But why? Mr. Larson is the biggest landowner around here. What else could he want?"

Joe chuckled. "He could want whatever it is he doesn't have, that's what!"

Lem shook his head. "I never cared for Hammond, but I can't believe he would stoop to killing somebody."

Joe's face grew hard. "Remember, his foreman killed Andy Leland."

Chapter Ten

Joe drew a deep breath. "Maybe I'm wrong, but take a look at what's happened. You had a good business here, then Larson started hauling his own goods." He turned to Ellen. "Has he taken any of your customers?"

Ellen chewed on her bottom lip. "Some stayed, but we lost a few."

"All right, now think about it. Ira and me come to work for you. All of a sudden he thinks that maybe, just maybe your business will make it, especially after you pay ahead on the mortgage. What other reason could he have for buying your note? And if the truth was known, the bank probably made a nice profit on the sale."

The older man looked up at his daughter. "Makes sense to me."

Frustration edged Ellen's voice. "But why us?"

Joe shook his head. "It isn't just you. Your father said a rancher." He turned to Lem. "Who was it, the Bar M?"

"Yeah. Madden, S.T. Madden. Biggest around besides Larson."

"That's the one. He's been having trouble."

Ellen spoke up. "Why, he had almost a hundred head rustled a couple weeks back, just before you left for Waco. We didn't hear about it for a couple days."

"She's right," exclaimed Lem.

Ira broke in. "Joe. Them cow tracks on the other side of Valley Mills. Remember them?"

"What cow tracks?" Lem looked around.

Rocking forward in his chair, Joe explained, "Looked like fifty to a hundred head cut across the road, from south to north."

The older man grew excited. "Other side of Valley Mills?"

"Yeah."

"Why, the Bar M is back southeast of Valley Mills. According to S.T., three or four hundred head were scattered all over. When they finally got all of them back together a couple days later, they were about a hundred short."

"Yes," Ellen put in. "S.T. figured they'd just wandered away or fallen down some of the ravines."

Lem rolled his chair closer to Joe. "You best tell Jess Lewis about them tracks, son. He'd like to know. Maybe he can run them owlhoots down."

Joe pushed to his feet. "Tell you what. Let's take a break. I'll see the sheriff, and then when I get back, we'll start planning our next move."

From behind the dingy saloon window, Henry Clay Brocius watched Joe Phoebe cross the muddy street and head for the sheriff's office. He narrowed his eyes, wondering what business the lean cowpoke had with the sheriff.

He glanced over his shoulder at Kraut, who was sitting

at the poker table with Navajo Dave, Kid Pecos, and Curly Franklin. It was time to put his plan into motion. He gestured to Kraut, who laid down his cards and lumbered across the room. "Yeah, boss?"

"That cowhand that walloped you, Joe Phoebe."

Kraut's blue eyes turned to ice. "I remember."

Brocius gestured out the window. "I just saw him go into the sheriff's office. I hear he's been bragging about how he whipped you."

The heavyset German grunted. He'd heard nothing like that, but if Brocius said it was true, then it was.

Brocius continued, "If I was in your shoes, I wouldn't want some drifter poking fun at me."

Kraut narrowed his eyes and doubled his fists. "Ain't nobody going to make fun of me. Nobody."

Joe emerged from the sheriff's office.

With a curt laugh, Brocius said, "Well, now's your time to do something about it. There he is."

Kraut glared out the window. He clenched and unclenched his fists. Not forgetting the last beating he suffered at Brocius' fists for acting without orders, he looked up at the burly foreman. "You mean it?"

Brocius stared at the dim-witted gunny. "Yeah. I mean it."

Just as the rawhide tough young cowpoke stepped over a water-filled rut in the street, a guttural voice called out to him.

"You! Joe Phoebe!"

Joe halted and looked around.

Kraut Meyer stood in the street at the base of stairs that led to the boardwalk in front of the Red Hand Saloon, his fat hand poised over the butt of his six-gun.

Joe's dark eyes grew cold. "That's me."

"I heard what you been saying. I aim to make sure you don't say it no more. Draw!"

The lean young man didn't move.

"I told you to draw!" Kraut shouted.

By now, a crowd had gathered on the boardwalk on either side of the muddy street.

A faint sneer curled Joe's thin lips. Hands held out to his side, he took a step toward Kraut. "Everybody's watching, Kraut. I'm not drawing. Shoot me, and you'll hang."

Swallowing hard, the fat German glanced nervously around.

Joe continued walking slowly toward him. "I don't know what you've heard, but it didn't come from me. I haven't given you no thought at all since the other night."

Kraut licked his lips. "I told you to draw!" he shouted once again.

"You don't want that, Kraut." By now, Joe was less than ten feet from the blustering owlhoot. He continued closing the distance between them. "You're not so dumb that you don't know I'm close enough that you'll catch lead too."

"I don't care. I don't need no one to make a fool out of me."

Snickers came from the onlookers. Kraut's ears burned. He clenched his teeth and grabbed for his revolver.

Faster than a striking snake, Joe's hand leaped out and grabbed the surprised German's wrist, twisting it aside and flinging the six-gun into one of the water-filled ruts. In the next instant, Joe backhanded the beefy German, knocking his battered Stetson from his bald head. Quicker than the eye could follow, Joe kicked Kraut on the side of his left knee, knocking his leg out from under him. Joe instantly shifted weight, whipping his free foot up, slamming the top of his instep into the falling man's chin.

Kraut's head popped back. His body followed, and the bulky outlaw slammed back into the mud, unconscious. Blood ran down the sides of his lips.

A light rain began to fall. Joe looked up, and his eyes met those of Henry Clay Brocius. He cut his gaze to the rain-filled bellies of the dark clouds overhead. With a wry edge to his voice, he said, "Best get your man inside. He'll get wet out here."

From the window in the freight office, Lem watched in wide-eyed amazement as Joe quickly and efficiently put Kraut on the ground. He looked up at Ira, who had witnessed the brief fight also. "I never seen anything like that. Where'd Joe learn that kind of fighting?"

Ira grunted. "He don't know. We talked about it once just after we left the Army. We was bullwhacking out of West Virginia when a couple hardcases tried to rob us in a back alley at Smithfield Crossing. He done that same kind of fighting. He said he don't remember where he learnt it. It just sort of come natural to him."

Red Coggins and Charley Lasater watched the brief fight from behind the batwings of the Leon Saloon next door to the tonsorial parlor. When Red saw how easily Joe disposed of Kraut Meyer, he whispered under his breath, "No doubt in my mind now, Charley. That jasper is Billy Reno. We ain't going to let him out of our sight."

Scratching his scraggly beard, Charley grunted. "What makes you so sure?"

Red ran the tip of his tongue along the gaps between his teeth. "The way he fought. He was around fifteen or so when his brother, Frank, found him and bought him from the Apache. That's their kind of kick fighting. I seen Billy do it once up in Palo Pinto when a bully tried to push him around."

That night at supper, Lem slurped at his coffee. "I been figuring about our next step. With what we got for the hides, and what we got in the bank, we're twenty-five hundred shy of what we need."

Ellen's face grew taut with concern.

Turning to her, Lem continued, "Next week is our regular run to Waco. Knowles Mercantile down in Baineye Creek and Shepp's up in Abbottville have big shipments coming in." He looked at his daughter. "I'm too crippled up to make the trip, but I'm going to send you to see George Weatherby at the First National Bank in Waco about a loan against the line. I know George. He knows what kind of business we have. Joe, you take her with you. Ira can stay here and help run the place."

Joe wasn't too crazy about the idea. It wasn't that he didn't like Ellen; he did, but he'd never spent much time with women. Being on the road with one for almost two weeks was almost more than he could imagine. He forced a faint smile. "Whatever you say, boss. If that's okay with Miss Ellen," he added in deference to her gender.

If the idea of two weeks unchaperoned with Joe Phoebe bothered her, she showed no sign. "If that's what you want, Pa." She turned to Joe. "I'll pack. We can pull out first thing in the morning."

Her Pa looked at Joe. "Fine. Joe, you go lay out the new

traces while I go over with Ira what we got going on around here the next couple weeks."

Ira snorted. "I hope you don't figure I'm going to do no cooking, Lem."

The old man shivered. "Lord no. You're probably worse than me in the kitchen. Colley'll take care of all that. You'll be busy enough. I picked up a couple horses I figure will fit in with the teams. You can break them in."

Joe disappeared into the barn while Ellen retired to her room to pack. Ira and Colley remained in the office with Lem, discussing the most pressing duties around the freight line.

While Joe laid out the traces, his mind went back to Billy Reno and the robbery in Abbottville. Knowing he and Ellen had to stop at Shepp's in Abbottville to pick up any Waco shipments, he decided to pay a visit to the sheriff there. Maybe he had been around when the bank was robbed.

Later, after Ellen excused herself for bed, Ira and Joe sat at the stove with Lem, smoking their cigarettes, sipping on the last of the older man's bonded bourbon he'd ordered from Kentucky the previous year, and discussing events of the last few weeks.

"I wish the sheriff had been in so I could have talked to him. I still think I'm right about Larson," Joe insisted.

"Yeah," Ira chimed in. "Somebody probably put Kraut up to that fight today."

Joe's eyes glittered with amusement. "What fight?"

Ira joined the laughter. "Just like the old joke: two blows struck, one when you struck him, and the other when he struck the ground."

Lem roared, then grew serious. "I got to agree with you, Joe. There's a heap more here than meets the eye."

A sharp knock at the office door interrupted them.

"It's open!" shouted Lem.

Sheriff Lewis pushed open the door, a hard look in his eyes and a cold expression on his face. "Sorry to bother you this late, but it's important."

"No trouble, Jess. What can I do for you?"

He fixed his eyes on Joe and held out a skinning knife with a bone handle. "Recognize this?"

Joe and Ira exchanged surprised looks. Joe took it from the sheriff and turned it over and over in his hand. "It's mine. I lost it on the last trip up to Waco." He looked up at the sheriff. "Where did you find it?"

Sheriff Lewis took the knife back and slipped it under his belt. "In Kraut Meyer's back. He's dead, and you're under arrest."

Chapter Eleven

Unable to believe his ears, Joe blinked several times. "What is this, a joke?"

His jaw set, the sheriff replied, "You're under arrest, Joe. Now come peaceable. Don't make me get tough."

Ira stepped forward, his eyes narrowing in suspicion. "Hold on, Sheriff. What's going on here?"

Lewis cut his eyes sharply at the old Johnny Reb. "Stay out of it, Ira. Kraut's dead. Joe's knife was found in his back. I'm arresting Joe until the judge arraigns him."

Ira looked around at Joe. "Brocius," he exclaimed. "This is Brocius' work."

Joe forced himself to remain calm. "Listen, Sheriff. On the way to Waco, we met Brocius at the Abbottville Cut-off." He quickly explained how the knife came to be missing and Brocius' threat to him and Ira. "That's the only answer. Brocius took the knife." Another thought struck him. "And the fight with Kraut this afternoon. I wager my last dollar Brocius egged him on me. And when that didn't work, that sidewinder used the knife, putting the blame on me. That way, he gets rid of me one way or another."

"That's right, Jess," Lem said. "Joe went over to see you today. You wasn't there, but he was going over to tell you about a heap of tracks on the other side of Valley Mills. They could be those made by S.T.'s rustled cattle. Kraut jumped him on the way back."

Ellen emerged from the adjoining room, her housecoat pulled around her. "What's happening?" She looked at her father. "Pa?"

Lem held up his hand for her to listen.

The sheriff said, "I heard about that—I mean about Kraut bracing him—but that don't make no mind. Like it or not, Lem, the evidence points to Joe. I don't make the decisions. It's up to the judge, but I wouldn't be much of a friend if I didn't tell you it don't look none too good for Joe. After all, a dozen old boys heard him in the saloon tell Kraut he'd kill him. Why, I even heard him say so myself."

"Now, slow down, Sheriff," Ira drawled. "When was this all supposed to have happened?"

"Sometime after supper. They found Kraut out behind your barn."

Ira grunted. "Joe couldn't have done it. He's been with us all night. There's three of us will swear to that fact."

The sheriff hesitated. He looked from one to the other. "Is that right, Lem? Was Joe with you all evening?"

Lem hesitated. He shot Joe a glance, remembering when he had sent the young man out to the barn to lay out the traces for the next morning.

Before he could answer, Joe spoke. "No, Sheriff. Not all evening. I went out in the barn to get the gear ready to pull out in the morning."

A mixture of both regret and gratitude showed in the old freight owner's eyes.

Jess turned to the older man. "That right, Lem?"

Slowly he nodded, his craggy face aging ten years.

Joe's brain raced, sorting his options quickly, coolly. If he permitted the sheriff to lock him up, a hemp party would soon follow, and he'd be doing a ballet at the end of a rope. No, the only way he could haul himself out of this mess was on his own.

He shucked his Paterson Colt. "Hold it right there, Sheriff. Don't move a muscle."

The sheriff gave Joe a wry grin. "Now, don't start that, Joe." He held out a hand. "Give me the pistol and come along peaceable."

The chill in Joe's voice froze the sheriff. "There's nothing to start, Sheriff. I don't want to hurt you, but if you force me, I will. The way the cards are stacked against me, I got no choice." Without taking his eyes off the sheriff, he shoved his knife under his belt. "Colley, go saddle the black for me. Ira, get the sheriff's gun and tie him up good. Ellen, tie your father so the wheels can't move."

They all looked at him in disbelief.

The warning in his voice left them no doubt. "When I leave here, all of you are going to be tied tighter than an old maid's corset."

With an amused gleam in his eyes, Ira did as Joe said.

Five minutes later, Joe snugged down the last knot around Ellen's wrists and leaned close to her ear. "I'll be in touch," he whispered.

Joe swung into the saddle, noting the bulging saddle-bags and thick bedroll tied behind the cantle of the saddle.

Not only had Colley saddled his horse, but the young man had packed grub and his soogan for him.

He headed east along the starlit road, his head filled with a dozen conflicting ideas. His first step was to find a secure spot from which to carry out the almost impossible task of not only learning the truth about Hammond Larson but also finding proof that Henry Clay Brocius murdered Kraut Meyer.

Just beyond the narrow road to the Circle L and well before the Abbottville Cutoff, the Waco road climbed through a mile-long pass of rocky crags that extended several miles back to the north, the Bittersweets, twenty square miles of rocky gorges, vast canyons with cold streams, all alive with wild game and deadly predators. He reined the black horse across the rocky ground and into a tableland covered by a maze of rugged boulders and jagged crags.

Being new to the country, Joe knew he was at a disadvantage in selecting a hideout, especially in the dim starlight. Those who followed him, and he was positive there would be many, were much more familiar with the countryside and aware of many of the natural refuges in which a man could hide.

After thirty minutes of wending his way through the vast field of boulders and crags, Joe pulled into a cul-de-sac that offered protection on three sides. According to the North Star, it was around three or four o'clock.

Dismounting, he hobbled the stallion and unsaddled him, then tossed his saddlebags and bedroll on the ground. Sleep was the last thing on his mind. He made a cigarette and, cupping his hands to hide the flare, touched a match to it.

He couldn't help noticing the wind swept the smoke in every direction. A smile split his angular face. Even if someone picked up the smell of cigarette smoke, he'd have no idea from which direction it came.

As false dawn lit the eastern sky, Joe climbed to the crest of the rocky canyon and studied the country around him. He needed an out-of-the-way hideout from where he could not only see the road, but also have a handy back door.

From where he stood, he spotted a granite ledge covered with boulders a quarter mile distant and about three hundred feet higher. It had a view of the road. *Now,* he told himself, *let's see what else it has to offer.*

An hour later, after looking over the spot, Joe decided it would be sufficient for a couple of days until he could find another refuge. Three or four hideaways would be better. That way, he wouldn't be returning to the same one each night.

The clatter of hoofbeats broke the silence of the still morning air. Joe ducked behind a boulder.

Down below to the west, a dozen riders pounded around a bend in the road. Sheriff Lewis was in the lead. Joe recognized some of the posse members as local citizens. His blood ran cold when he spotted three of Brocius' men riding in the posse.

He shook his head grimly. The burly foreman wasn't planning on taking any chances.

The posse pounded past but returned minutes later, searching the rocky ground. Joe grimaced. The sheriff was no greenhorn in tracking.

When Joe saw Sheriff Lewis instructing the posse to

search different areas of the rugged canyon, he realized Lewis had cut his sign, so he decided to take the back door he'd discovered and lose himself deep into the rugged forest of oak and hickory and sweet gum.

Twenty minutes later, just before he rode out of the tableland of crags and boulders, he heard voices ahead. Muttering a soft curse at how the posse had managed to circle him so quickly, he led his horse along a winding passage. The trail forked in half a dozen different directions. He took one that angled back deeper into the field of giant boulders. Ahead a tangle of wild azaleas blocked half of the narrow path.

Joe started to push past, but then he discovered the thick underbrush also covered the mouth of another trail. Moving the branches gently, he led his horse into the new trail, where it ended in a small cave.

A quarter mile distant, Red Coggins reined up. He scratched his head. "Reckon we missed a bet here."

Charley grunted. "Yep. If Reno had been in these rocks, the posse would have flushed him out, right into our hands."

Red pursed his lips. "Right into the hands that would help him escape."

"That was sure a smart idea, Red."

The slight grifter shrugged. "You figure. Running from the law, he's got to go for the gold. We can find him first and convince him we're on his side."

"Yeah," chuckled Charley. "I see what you mean."

For the next two hours, the posse scoured the badland of crags and rocks without a trace of Joe Phoebe.

The sounds of the search faded away. Joe remained

silent, unmoving for another hour before venturing from his refuge. Once or twice, his stallion had jittered about nervously. He pinched the animal's nostrils and ran his hand over the nervous horse's neck, all the while speaking in soft, soothing tones.

The silence settling over the rugged crags sent a wave of relief surging through Joe's veins. There was no question, however, that the posse would return. Shading his eyes with his hand, he noted the sun had maybe an hour or two before it dropped beneath the horizon.

Joe had long stopped questioning his own reactions or decisions, attributing them instead to the training and experience he acquired before he lost his memory.

He couldn't tell you how he knew, but with a certainty, he understood that one hand between the sun and the horizon was an hour. Two hands, two hours. Each finger, fifteen minutes.

Same with his magic with horses. He could not remember how or where he gained the knack, the skill, but he possessed it. Nor had he any explanation for his fighting techniques. The skills came naturally, as if he had practiced them for years.

Ever since he awakened in the hospital in West Virginia, he often felt like a stranger walking around in another man's body. He wasn't, but the feeling persisted. Over time, it had diminished somewhat, but never to the point that he was unaware of the eerie sensation of being another person.

An hour before sunset, he decided to find another lair in which he would be safe. His stomach growled. He'd had nothing to eat since the previous day. Well, the stomach could wait. If nothing else, he'd just tighten his belt a couple of notches, what the old timers called a Spanish supper. He needed a refuge first, then he could dig into the grub Colley had packed.

Chapter Twelve

Thirty minutes after he left the cave, Joe ran across a stream of icy water coursing down a cobbled bed of limestone. In one pool, he spotted several fish swimming about lazily. While his horse grazed, he quickly hacked a slender willow down and fashioned a spear.

Minutes later, he rode out, two fat bass on a strip of rawhide dangling from his saddle horn. Another thirty minutes, he built a small fire, broiled the fish, and then rode out.

Just before dark, he spotted a growth of ancient cedars at the base of a sheer wall of limestone. Within the thick motte of conifers, he made a cold camp.

Next morning, Joe headed for the Circle L, Hammond Larson's spread. In his gut, he knew the wealthy rancher had ordered Brocius to get rid of him, and Kraut Meyer's murder was the means to do so.

And he knew why. Larson didn't want Joe or Ira around to help bail Lem Mills and his family out of the financial bind in which he had placed them by buying up their note from Banker Phares.

Now his job was to find indisputable proof that Brocius killed Kraut, proof that would help the law nail Hammond Larson's slimy skin to the post.

First he needed supplies. He had just about polished off the canned peaches and corn dodgers Colley had hurriedly stuffed into the saddlebags. Abbottville was the closest village. He knew he was taking a risk on riding in, for not only was the Circle L nearby, but he had also unloaded freight at Shepp's Mercantile and the blacksmith's only two weeks earlier. Still, it was a chance he had to take.

Red Coggins had the same notion about stocking up. He had no idea how long they would be out searching for Billy Reno, so he sent Charley into Abbottville for grub while he continued to cast about the forest for any sign of their prey.

Shepp's Mercantile carried everything from saddles to Needham's Tonic, pickles to corn seed, bolt cloth to long johns, black powder to .44 rimfires.

Charley had just finished paying for his grub when Joe walked in and bellied up to the counter. The slight owlhoot could only gape at Joe, who glanced at him. Ears burning, Charley quickly left the mercantile, scurrying to hide at the edge of town so he could follow Joe Phoebe, the real Billy Reno.

After Charley left, Joe realized he had met the drifter sometime back when he and Ira were hauling buffalo hides to Waco. They were the hombres who remarked how much he looked like Billy Reno. And, he reminded himself, they also said they were taking care of business at the Abbott-ville Bank, then moving on.

Moving on? Then what was this one doing still around?

Joe watched as Charley rode south out of town and disappeared around the first bend in the road.

The hair on the back of his neck bristled. He scratched at it, then turned back to the proprietor behind the counter and slid his supplies into his saddlebags. "What do I owe you?"

Outside, Joe deliberately took his time tying his saddlebags to his saddle, cutting his eyes back to the bend in the south road around which the gap-toothed range bum had disappeared. He couldn't help wondering what had kept those two drifters around so long.

At the same time, Curly Franklin sauntered out the batwing doors of the Abbottville Emporium and paused on the boardwalk. He surveyed the small village idly. He froze when he spotted Joe swinging into his saddle across the street. He darted back inside and gestured for Navajo Dave. "Get over here," he hissed.

By the time Dave reached Curly's side, Joe was riding north out of town.

"Let's get him," Dave said, pushing through the doors. "That's the one what killed Kraut."

Before they could mount, Charley Lasater rode past, his eyes fixed on the bend around which Joe had vanished.

Sitting on the black stallion back in the woods, Joe clenched his teeth as he watched the small owlhoot ride back through town in his direction.

His face grew hard when he spotted Curly and Navajo

Dave following Charley. Quickly he dismounted and led the stallion into a dense thicket. The plans he had for Charley would have to wait.

A few minutes later, Charley rode past. Shortly, muted voices came from the road. Joe strained to hear them. As the riders drew nearer, their voices became clearer.

"I'm going to make that jasper pay for what he done to Kraut," said Navajo Dave.

"I never figured you cared much for the German," Curley teased.

His voice brusque, the Navajo said, "Maybe not, but he was my partner. Yours too."

"I feel the same way. The only way I can figure that Phoebe could knife Kraut is if he caught the German drunk."

Dave snorted. "That's probably what happened. Kraut was no slouch with a knife."

Joe's brows furrowed in surprise, then bewilderment. If he understood what he overheard, the gang members also believed he had killed Kraut.

By now, the voices were distant murmurs. Leading the stallion back to the road, he turned back to Abbottville. Best he could recollect, Larson's place was back southeast of the village.

The winding road between Abbottville and Reys Fort marked the property lines between Madden's Bar M and the Circle L.

Joe reined up at the cutoff to the Circle L. The sun would be down in a couple of hours. He decided to keep riding until he found a secure camp, then he could return the next day. Ahead, the country grew rougher. Sprawling valleys of lush graze gave way to rugged hills and canyons.

Joe made an early camp beneath a slab of limestone deep in a canyon, which appeared to be the center of a warren of trails leading off in every direction.

For the first time since the night he fled Dead Apache Springs, he allowed himself the luxury of coffee and bacon, after which he doused the fire well before the sun set.

As he lay on his blanket, he thought back to the conversation between Brocius' two hired guns. They had no way of knowing they were being overheard, so they had no reason to fabricate any of their conversation. Chances were, Kid Pecos and the other riders of the Circle L believed the same way, that Joe Phoebe had murdered Kraut.

Brocius was sure playing this hand close to the vest. He wasn't even letting his own gunhands know what he was doing. With a wry grin, Joe spoke softly into the darkness. "Slick. Mighty slick."

Chapter Thirteen

With the setting of the sun, a soft rain began to fall, a gentle, steady drizzle to set the grass and fill the waterholes. Well before sunup, the south wind blew away the clouds, leaving the countryside bright and glistening, refreshed and ready to battle another simmering Central Texas day.

After gnawing on cold bacon and sipping the last of his cold coffee, Joe rode out with the rising sun, heading back to the Circle L. The rain had washed all tracks from the road.

He rode the winding road warily, his eyes constantly quartering the countryside around him. As he approached a rugged canyon, the black stallion stiffened, his ears perking forward.

Joe reined up and shucked his Paterson Colt.

From beyond the finger of the boulder-strewn canyon, a cowboy dressed in black rode out. When he spotted Joe, he jerked his sorrel to a halt and laid his hand on his own six-gun. "Hold on, partner!" he called out. "I ain't looking for no trouble."

Joe didn't recognize the stranger. He forced a smile. "I didn't know anyone was around."

"You caught me by surprise too. I'd camped back in here last night to get out of the rain. Name's Jimmy Jack McGinnis from Arizona Territory by way of San Antone. Some folks call me Jimmy the Deuce."

Slowly, Joe holstered his Colt. "Howdy. I'm Bill Smith."

Recognizing the name was a lie, a knowing smirk played over Jimmy the Deuce's thin lips. "Howdy, Bill." He pointed up the road. "I'm heading thataway. Want to ride along?"

"For a piece."

They fell in together. Jimmy the Deuce was a garrulous galoot who could put a mockingbird to shame. "Got me a job with the Circle L. Supposed to be around here somewhere. You know where it is?"

Every muscle grew tense. Joe shook his head. "No. Just riding in myself." He paused. "Punching cows?"

The slender man laughed. "Punching cows? Not me." He held up his right hand, flexing his slender and delicate fingers. "Give me a deck of cards or a six-gun, and I'm right to home. But punching cows? That ain't for me."

"This job you mentioned. Reckon they need any other hands?"

Jimmy glanced at Joe's Paterson. "Reckon if you're good with that hogleg. I heard they was having trouble down in a place called Dead Apache Springs. You heard of that?"

Joe hesitated as if he were thinking. "Nope. Never heard of it." At the same time, he was telling himself he had to inform Lem and Ira that Larson had another gunfighter coming in, and this one looked mighty dangerous.

Jimmy continued, "Don't know exactly what the trouble is, but when someone wants to hire a gun, it ain't for no ice-cream supper." The lean gunman reined up and dismounted. He checked the sorrel's front left foot and popped a pebble from under the shoe and one from the groove of the frog. He cursed. "Blaze here is a fine pony, but he gets sore feet mighty easy."

They rode out of the rugged canyons and down into the lush valleys, where Jimmy the Deuce pointed to a sign beside a narrow trail cutting off the main road. "That's the place," he said. "Circle L Ranch." He looked around at Joe. "You going to ride on in about a job?"

Joe shook his head. "Reckon not. I'm no hand with a six-gun unless it's going after rattlesnakes."

Jimmy touched a slender finger to the brim of his hat. "You take care, you hear?"

"You too."

Joe continued along the road until the gunman in black disappeared from view. He planned on cutting northwest through the forest as soon as he could, hoping to hit the Circle L Road to Dead Apache Springs. He didn't want to take a chance on running into Red Coggins or Charley Lasater up around Abbottville. After another mile, he cut off the road, taking as direct a route as he could manage.

He had been on the run only a short time, not enough time for Larson to get word out to Jimmy the Deuce. That meant the rancher sent for the gunfighter a few weeks back, about the time Joe and Ira hired on with Lem.

That night, Joe tied the stallion back in the forest behind the livery barn. Ghosting through the darkness, he slipped into the corral and disappeared into the deep shadows in the barn.

A light shone from the freight office. Joe peered through a rear window and let out a sigh of relief when he spotted Ira and the others about the desk. Softly, he tapped on the back door and then slipped inside, kneeling behind a table. "Quick. Close the front shade."

Colley hurried across the office and closed the shade.

Outside, Hymie Swartz, the town barber and undertaker, paused on the boardwalk when the shade went down. He scratched his balding head. Lem never closed the front shade. He spotted a small gap between the shade and window jamb. A nosy little man, he peered through the gap just as Joe rose from behind the table and shook Ira Croton's hand vigorously. Swartz's eyes grew wide. Phoebe! Joe Phoebe was back in town.

It was all over town how Phoebe had tied up the sheriff and the others before fleeing. Now he was back! Hastily, Hymie backed off the boardwalk and scurried across the street to the sheriff's office.

Ellen scowled. "What are you doing here? It's too dangerous."

Her father hushed her.

"How you been, partner?" Ira asked.

Colley stood at the window, peering out the gap, his ears taking in the hurried conversation.

"I'm fine," Joe whispered. He looked at Ellen. "What are you doing here? I thought you were going to Waco for a loan."

"She is," Lem interrupted. "Her and Ira is pulling out day after tomorrow. They're taking their ponies. Deliveries can wait. What with the murder and all, things have been mighty nervous here in town."

"Yeah," Colley exclaimed over his shoulder. "We even had some prowlers around last night."

Ellen gestured to Ira. "And some of Brocius' boys gave Ira some trouble until the sheriff came over and put a stop to it."

"It wasn't nothing," Ira said hastily. "Just talk. Bragging on their side about what they would do when they caught you." He shook his head. "You shouldn't be here. Kraut's death is the talk of town. The undertaker kept him in the window until today when they buried him."

"I'm leaving," Joe said. "But the reason I come is that Larson hired another gunfighter. Jimmy the Deuce. Looks dangerous."

Lem whistled softly. "I've heard of that owlhoot. He is dangerous as a grizzly."

"You need anything, partner? Grub, ammunition?"

"Nope. Picked up a stake of supplies in Abbottville yesterday. If you need—"

Colley interrupted, "The sheriff!" He looked around in alarm, his eyes wide as a stepped-on toad frog. "The sheriff's coming with Deputy Rennig."

Lem grimaced. "Where's the other deputy? Rufus?"

"Don't see him, Pa."

Joe reached for the rear door. "You need me, come to the Abbottville Cutoff at noon. I'll make sure to drop by every day. Don't wait more than a half hour or so if I don't show."

Ira hurried across the room. "Get out of here." He grabbed the door and followed Joe into the barn. "Hurry!"

Joe hesitated. "Take care going to Waco."

"Yeah, yeah. Git! Blast it! Git out of here!"

Outside, Joe Phoebe climbed through the corral rails. A harsh voice growled. "Hold it right there, Phoebe!"

Back inside, Ira closed the door behind him just as the sheriff and Deputy Chester Rennig burst in, guns drawn. They looked around the room hurriedly. The sheriff shouted, "Where is he? Where's Joe Phoebe?"

Lem looked up from his desk. "Phoebe? Why, Jess, what makes you think he'd be here?"

"That's right, Sheriff," purred Ellen. "We haven't seen him since he left us all tied up here."

An excited voice echoed through the rear door. "Sheriff! Sheriff! Out here. I got Joe Phoebe!"

Deputy Rufus Bird gestured with the muzzle of his six-gun. "All right, Phoebe. Turn around and put your hands up."

As Joe turned, his foot lashed out, sending the six-gun spinning into the darkness. He spun around, and when he came out of the spin, he threw a straight right into the startled deputy's jaw, dropping him on the ground unconscious.

Moments later, astride the black stallion, he thundered onto the street and out of town.

The next morning, Hammond Larson called Brocius into his home office on the Circle L. "I learned yesterday at the bank that Ellen Mills and that Johnny Reb hired hand are heading for Waco, pulling out tomorrow. The old man figures he can get a loan up there." From his experience with the coldhearted rancher, Brocius sensed what was coming next.

Larson studied him. "A new man came in yesterday. Jimmy the Deuce."

"I met him," Brocius grunted.

"Get him. I've been playing easy so far, but now it's time to get rough. I don't want them to reach the bank. Persuade them to turn back."

The burly foreman narrowed his eyes, knowing exactly what his boss meant by persuade. "Yes, sir, Mr. Larson."

Chapter Fourteen

Stunted cedar grew high in the rugged limestone crags overlooking the Abbottville Cutoff. Chewing on bacon and bread, Joe watched from behind the conifers as Sheriff Lewis led a posse east along the road.

A faint smile played over his thin lips, and his dark eyes glittered with amusement. Jess Lewis might not be a greenhorn as a tracker, but with all the signs in the road, only a savvy pathfinder could follow a single trail. And the sheriff was not that savvy. The posse split at the cutoff, half continuing east, the others south.

Poking the last of the bacon in his mouth, Joe used his knife to open a can of peaches and washed the bacon and bread down with sweet juice. With the posse on the prowl, he had to remain hidden until they gave up the search in the area.

The posse met at the Abbottville Cutoff around mid-afternoon and turned back to Dead Apache Springs to the west. Waiting until they were out of sight, Joe pulled onto the narrow road and headed east toward Valley Mills, intent on picking up the cattle trail he and Ira had spotted on their trip to Waco.

While several storms had almost obliterated the tracks, the bovines had left enough cow patties that Joe could follow at a trot.

The lean cowboy grew cautious as the trail led into rough country. He made his way slowly beneath serrated ridges that threatened to split the belly of the blue sky and through deep canyons choked with underbrush thick enough to hide a good-size pony less than ten feet off the trail.

The sky was clear as fresh springwater, filled with the calls of blue jays, the *tap-tap-tap*ping of red-bellied woodpeckers, and the beating wings of startled bobwhites put to flight. Off to the south, darting sparrows chased a red-tailed hawk. In the distance came the soft lowing of cattle.

Pulling well off the trail deep into the thick vegetation, Joe dismounted and slipped forward on foot. Around a long finger of boulders, he discovered a box canyon. Sapling logs blocked the canyon mouth. Beyond grazed a herd of cows and horses.

Joe scanned the rugged country around him just to make certain he was alone before climbing between the gate poles into the canyon. Inside he discovered several different brands, the majority of which was Bar M, S.T. Madden's brand. Half a dozen ponies stared at him curiously. Down to the last one, they carried the Circle L mark.

Satisfied, he turned to leave when he heard voices. He shucked his sixgun and ducked behind a thick hedge of elderberry growing against the canyon wall near the pole gate. Curly and Navajo Dave rode up.

"I don't know why Brocius has to see about these beeves so much. They can't get out."

The Navajo turned up a half-empty bottle of whiskey and chugged a couple of swallows. "Don't gripe so much, Curly. Here. Take a drink. It'll make you feel better."

Joe stiffened. So that was Curly.

Pausing at the gate, Dave dropped two of the rails and rode in. Curly replaced the rails and vanished with him back among the stolen cows.

Moving soundlessly, Joe hurried back to the black stallion. By the time he reached the Waco road, the sun was setting.

Two hours later, he pulled into his camp up in the Bittersweets.

The next morning, Joe watched as two riders rounded the bend west of the Abbottville Cutoff. From his perch high on a rugged crag, he recognized Ira and Ellen, who was wearing trousers and handling her sorrel mare like she had been born to the saddle.

Joe considered stopping them, but instead he cupped his hand to his mouth and gave the sharp shrill cry—*whip-poo-weee*, *whip-poo-weee*, *whip-poo-weee*—of the whip-poor-will.

Down below, Ira glanced up among the crags. Ellen followed his gaze in alarm. "What is it? You see something?"

The old Johnny Reb turned his face away from the young woman and loosed a stream of tobacco. "No, ma'am," he said, turning back. "But that's Joe up there. He's watching us."

Her face lit with excitement. "Where?" She reined up.

"You can't see him," Ira said, continuing down the road. "But he's up there."

Pressing her knees gently into the mare's ribs, she sent the animal after Ira, glancing back up at the forbidding crags, an unexpected feeling of excitement surging through her veins.

Joe continued to watch the road. A couple of wagons passed heading for Dead Apache Springs; a handful of drifters cut down the Abbottville Road. His gaze ran down the narrow road in the direction of the Circle L.

Hammond Larson was behind the whole scheme, the rustling and Kraut's murder. Brocius was the only way Joe could get to Larson. And it would be harder to find hair on a frog than to drag a confession from the hardcase foreman. Joe drew a deep breath, trying to figure out his first step.

He immediately stiffened when he spotted Jimmy the Deuce emerge from the Abbottville Road and turn east in the same direction as Ira and Ellen. He was forking a gray horse, not the sorrel he had been riding when Joe met him.

His blood ran cold. Why was the killer heading east? Had he decided against working for Larson? That was hard to believe. Larson had the money, and that's what drove a killer like Jimmy the Deuce.

Joe swung into the saddle and picked his way down the precipitous slope to the road below. He'd learn for himself what Jimmy Jack McGinnis had in mind.

Joe remained in the forest, catching occasional glimpses of the road. Jimmy the Deuce seemed in no hurry.

* * *

Ira and Ellen kept their ponies in a steady trot. Jimmy the Deuce kept pace, coming within sight of the two in late afternoon. He reined back on his gray horse, pulling into a thick cluster of buttonballs lining the road.

Spotting the gunslinger behind the tangle of button-balls, Joe slowed his horse, waiting for the man in black to move out.

That evening, Ellen and Ira rode into Carolina, a small village some thirty miles outside of Waco. There were two inns. Ira pointed to the Carolina Inn. "Joe and me pulled in here for dinner one day. Purty clean. Got two or three ladies working there, so they'll probably have room for you, Miss Ellen."

"What about that one down the street, the Horse-shoe?"

Ira lifted an eyebrow. "We went in there once, but left quick as we could. An honest gent couldn't make it through one night in that place and come out alive."

Ellen was given a bed in the room with the proprietor's fifteen-year-old daughter. Ira bunked with three travelers. The rooms were clean and free of cooties.

Ira put up the animals while Ellen freshened up, and then they sat at one of a dozen small tables in the large room and enjoyed a filling meal of beef and vegetable stew; homemade bread, hot and buttered; and milk cooled in the stream out back.

Within minutes after the sun fell behind the forest, darkness enveloped the countryside. Stars filled the sky, illumining the rugged crags and spreading forests with a silvery blue light.

Joe watched as Jimmy the Deuce rode up to the inn, tied his pony to the hitching rail, and ambled inside.

Ira looked up when the door opened and a lean hard-case dressed in black stepped in and surveyed the room before heading to the bar and ordering a drink.

Ellen paid the newcomer no attention, but as soon as Ira spotted the gunny, he knew who he was. Dropping his hand unobtrusively to his Colt, he flipped the leather loop from the hammer.

The gunfighter tossed down half his whiskey, then turned and leaned back, resting his elbows on the bar. His cold eyes scanned the room, settling on Ira and Ellen.

After a few minutes, Ellen became aware that he was staring at them. Under her breath, she said. "Ira. That man at the bar. He—"

He interrupted her. "Don't look at him. Keep eating. That's the gunslinger Joe told us about, Jimmy the Deuce."

"But he's staring at us."

"Yes, ma'am, he most certainly is." From under his eyebrows, he watched the young woman across the table. Her gaze was on her plate, but Ira knew eating was the last thing on her mind.

Lifting a spoonful of stew to her lips, she whispered, "Is he looking for us?"

"Don't know for certain. Maybe so, but don't worry. He won't do nothing in here. His kind, they don't want no witnesses."

Her heart thudded in her chest. "What do we do now?"

"Act natural, like you finished your supper and you're going upstairs for bed."

When Ellen looked up, Ira saw the fear in her eyes, but he also saw the set in her jaw and the determination imprinted on her face. "You'll be all right, Miss Ellen. Now go on up."

Without looking in Jimmy the Deuce's direction, Ellen strode purposely across the crowded room and mounted the stairs. The sound of a closing door echoed through the inn.

The gunfighter pushed away from the bar. Carrying his tumbler of whiskey in his hand, he sauntered over to Ira's table, a smug sneer on his thin lips.

Ira slipped his Colt from its holster and laid it on his lap.

Jimmy the Deuce stopped at the table, looked down, then took a sip of whiskey. "You don't need the hogleg, old man. You'd be deader than a beaver hat before you could cock the trigger."

The old Johnny Reb narrowed his eyes. "It's already cocked."

The younger man chuckled. "I reckon I misjudged you. Won't make that mistake again. You work for Mills." It was a statement, not a question.

"Maybe." Ira shrugged.

An amused gleam shone in the gunfighter's eyes. "I come to tell you not to go on to Waco. Turn around and go back. I don't cotton to hurt a woman or an old man, especially one on whose side I fought in the War for Southern Independence."

His eyes growing cold, Ira replied, "If we go on?"

The killer grimaced. He downed the last of his drink and set the tumbler on the table. "You'll regret it. I promise you." He turned on his heel and disappeared out the door.

From where he watched from the shadows of a barn, Joe narrowed his eyes as Jimmy the Deuce swung into the saddle and headed east out of Carolina. Joe looked back at the inn, debating on whether he should contact Ira or not.

He could only guess what had taken place within the walls of the inn. He knew the killer had not followed Ira and Ellen such a distance just to say howdy. His own pulse racing, he decided to follow the hardened killer.

Chapter Fifteen

Ten minutes out of the small village, Joe stiffened in the saddle when he heard a horse whinny back in the forest. Eyes fixed forward, he continued east, the hair on the back of his neck tingling. Someone was watching. Jimmy the Deuce?

Hoping the killer hadn't recognized him, Joe continued east along the winding road for a quarter mile. He met two late-riding drifters heading for Carolina. They greeted him as they passed.

After they disappeared around a bend in the road, Joe pulled into the understory vegetation and dismounted on the edge of a grove of sweet gum trees. By now, the drifters' hoofbeats had faded down the road.

He picketed his stallion, then headed back through the forest, picking his way around the underbrush and berry briars, pausing frequently to listen to the sounds around him. Somewhere deep in the forest, a rabbit squealed, an owl cried out, a fox barked.

Not long after he and Ira had signed on to bullwhack

teams out of West Virginia, renegade Shawnees attacked
the wagons. Joe escaped into the forest, instinctively taking cover beneath a floor of dried leaves while the Shawnees scoured the area.

Later, he puzzled over how he knew what actions to
take, but finally dismissed the conundrum as one of the
many skills he possessed, the memory of which had been
lost when the minié ball slammed into his temple.

So now, utilizing that Indian stealth, he slipped like a
wraith through the forest in the direction of Jimmy the
Deuce. Moving slowly but unerringly, he froze when the
snuffle of a horse no more than twenty feet distant broke
the silence. Was this jasper the deadly gunfighter waiting
for Ira and Ellen? Or simply a drifter? When he heard
Jimmy's voice calming his pony, he had his answer.

He eased to his knees in the damp leaves behind the
massive trunk of an ancient live oak, and waited.

As the darkness faded into false dawn, Joe peered
around the trunk of the live oak, spotting Jimmy the
Deuce crouched behind the thick trunk of a long-fallen
oak some thirty feet away. The gunfighter was checking
his six-gun.

Distant hoofbeats broke the crisp morning air. Jimmy
Jack McGinnis pushed to his feet and holstered his six-
gun. He started for the road.

Joe Phoebe stepped from behind the live oak, his eyes
cold as ice and his jaw set like a slab of granite. "Hello,
Jimmy."

Jimmy the Deuce froze. With his hands held out to his
sides, he turned slowly. He squinted into the shadows cast
by the spreading live oak. A faint sneer curled his thin

lips. "Well, well, if it ain't Bill Smith, alias Joe Phoebe. Right?"

A crooked smile played over Joe's weather-beaten face. "Never liked lying to no one, but sometimes a body's got no choice." He paused and added, "Like now."

The lean gunslinger's eyes narrowed. "What do you have in mind, Joe?"

"Depends."

"On what?"

"On what you got in mind."

"I got a job to carry out. Done been paid."

Joe nodded to the sound of approaching hoofbeats. "That's the job?"

"Yep. They ain't going to no bank."

"Why don't you just ride back to the Circle L, Jimmy? Give Larson his money and head back to Arizona Territory."

"Can't. Got my reputation to think about."

Joe drew a deep breath and released it slowly. "Hate to hear that."

The sneer on Jimmy the Deuce's lips tightened. "That's the way life is, partner. Like it or not." The challenge in his tone was evident.

The hoofbeats were drawing closer.

Joe's eyes grew colder. "Well, then, Jimmy, I reckon you'll have to go through me." He paused. "From the sound, you don't have much time."

The sudden change in Joe's demeanor surprised the gunslinger. He tilted his head slightly, studying Joe Phoebe more closely. He saw the rawhide loop that normally lay over the hammer of the Paterson dangling against the worn leather of the holster. He had no idea just how handy

Joe might be with a six-gun, but he knew for sure the cold-eyed cowhand facing him had come to fight.

The killer chuckled. "In a way, it's a shame, Joe. Some other time, we might have been friends."

With a terse shake of his head, Joe replied, "I don't think so, Jimmy. I never had a hankering to crawl into a den of snakes."

A look of pure hatred crushed Jimmy the Deuce's slender face. "Why, you—" He clawed for his six-gun. He swung the barrel up. The last thing he saw was the cloud of smoke billowing from Joe's Paterson. He never even heard the booming report of the shot that hit him between the eyes.

On the road, the hoofbeats stopped abruptly. Joe stared down at the limp body dressed in black, then holstered his six-gun. He peered through the forest in the direction of the road, spying Ira and Ellen through the tangle of underbrush and low-hanging limbs. He called out, "Ira! It's me, Joe. Everything's all right."

The old Johnny Reb laughed and reined his pony into the forest. "I was wondering when you was going to show up." He frowned when he spotted the body. "That be who I think it is?"

"Yep." Behind Ira, Ellen strained to see what Ira was talking about. Joe hurried to her pony. "You don't need to look, Miss Ellen. It ain't a good thing to see," he added, leading her mare back to the road.

When Ira came up beside her, Joe explained, "Larson's hired gun. Jimmy the Deuce."

Ellen knit her brows. She looked up at Ira. "He's the one at the inn last night? The one you said warned us not to go on to Waco?"

"Yes, ma'am. He's the one."

Her dark eyes grew cold, and she set her jaw. "Will there be others?"

Grimacing, Joe hesitated. "Probably. When Larson finds out his man didn't do the job, he'll hire more."

She drew a deep breath, then released it slowly. With grim determination, she said, "Then we best get on to Waco before he finds out."

Joe looked up at Ira. "I'll take care of this body. You two get going. Keep your eyes peeled on the way back."

Scratching at the scraggly gray whiskers that had sprouted on his angular face over the last couple of days, Ira asked, "What about you?"

His dark eyes glittered in amusement. "Me? I'm going to try to keep Larson and Brocius so busy, they won't have time to think about you two."

Rifling through Jimmy the Deuce's pockets, Joe pulled out two hundred Yankee dollars. He tore them to shreds and stuffed them back in the dead gunfighter's shirt pocket. Then he draped the body over the killer's saddle, noting that the gray horse carried a Circle L brand. He headed back to Larson's spread, planning on riding all night to deliver an unexpected guest in time for the rancher's breakfast the next morning.

Staying on the side of the road, Joe pulled into the thick foliage each time he heard approaching travelers. He skirted Carolina, and just before sundown, as a row of thunderstorms rolled overhead, swung around Valley Mills.

Two miles east of the Abbottville Cutoff and Rattlesnake Hill, Joe reined up. He had planned to cut directly through the forest to the Circle L, but the forest was too dark. He'd have to wait until sunrise.

With the sun came another line of showers.

After climbing a tortuous pass, he topped out on an oblong mesa of jagged granite. The rain slackened as he crossed the crest of the mesa, following a trail that ran alongside a precipitous cutbank overlooking a coursing stream two hundred feet below. Joe reined up when the trail began its descent. In the distance, he spotted a sprawling rock house with barns and stables forming a semicircle around it.

The gray stallion trotted up beside Joe, its ears perked forward. The animal sensed its home.

From his vantage point high on the rugged escarpment, Joe scanned the countryside sprawling below. He could see for miles—cattle grazing, wranglers working scattered small herds, and cowpokes pushing animals into corrals. Veils of rain raced across the valley in his direction like galloping mustangs.

With a click of his tongue, he eased his stallion down the trail, the gray horse at his side. At the base of the mesa where the trail opened onto the lush meadows, he tied the reins about the gray horse's saddle horn and sent the animal trotting back to the ranch with its gruesome burden.

A shot cut through the patter of rain. Joe jerked his hands away as his saddle horn exploded. Two more shots rang out.

Chapter Sixteen

Henry Clay Brocius and three of his men burst from a motte of oak back to the east, their six-guns belching orange plumes and whining lead plums.

Driving rain struck like a hammer as Joe wheeled the stallion about and raced back up the rocky trail that was growing slipperier than calf slobber in the downpour. Slugs slammed in the rock on either side of him, ricocheting in a frightening shower of granite slivers.

The grim cowboy swore softly as he leaned over the neck of the galloping stallion. Thunder boomed like cannons, drowning out the pop of gunfire. An ear-splitting explosion of lightning nearby momentarily deafened him. His ears rang. Behind him, the staccato cracking of iron hooves against rock sounded like the deadly rattling of a Gatling gun.

"Keep it up, boy," Joe urged the stallion.

The horse's great strides ate up the ground. They topped out on the mesa and sped toward the trail on the far side. Just before reaching the trail leading down the mesa, Joe

shot a glance over his shoulder at his pursuers. A numb-
ing blow slammed into his forehead, knocking his back
against the galloping horse's lathered neck.

Joe clung instinctively to the animal, but when the racing black horse dipped down the trail, his grip began to
fail. He fought at the darkness threatening to swallow
him. His muscles refused to listen to his screaming brain.

A blast of rain struck.

Joe's fingers opened. He felt himself falling, striking
the ground so hard that stars exploded in his head. He
rolled a few feet, then abruptly dropped off the mesa rim,
vaguely aware of striking an object as he plummeted and
slammed to the ground.

He felt the rain on his face while at the same time he
sensed a great blackness enveloping him. Just before un-
consciousness closed about the wounded young cowpoke,
he rolled against the wall of the precipice from which he
had fallen.

Digging his spurs into his pony's flanks, Brocius had
charged across the mesa, spotting Joe Phoebe clinging to
the back of his stallion as a thick veil of blinding rain swept
over them, enveloping the stallion. "There he goes," Navajo
Dave shouted from behind. "Down the mesa!"

They raced through the downpour and down the mesa,
but by the time they reached the forest below, the horse
had vanished. Swearing mightily, Brocius reined up. "We'll
get him next time, boys." He reined about. "Now let's see
what Phoebe was up to."

By the time Brocius and his boys got back to the Circle
L, two of the wranglers had dragged Jimmy the Deuce

from the saddle and laid him out on the hay in the barn. Brocius' face grew hard when he saw the dead gunfighter and then turned to pure rage when one of the wranglers handed him the shredded currency.

Skillet, the cook, stuck his head out of the cook shack as Brocius left the barn. "Boss wants to see you!" he shouted, his voice a cackle.

Hammond Larson's square face was red as a pair of new long johns. He held a tumbler of bourbon in his hand, the glitter in his eyes mute evidence of how much whiskey he had tossed down even at this time of morning. When Brocius entered, Larson turned from the rain-streaked window and glared at him. "You see McGinnis?"

Slapping his wet hat against his batwing chaps, the foreman grunted. "Yep." His boss was furious, but the only one the rancher could blame was himself. He'd found and hired Jimmy the Deuce. Brocius dumped the torn currency on the desk. "This was in his pocket."

Larson glared at the pile of torn bills. "Why, that . . ." He exploded into a stream of invectives. "I can't believe that old man took him." He reached for the whiskey.

Brocius grunted. "The old man didn't do it."

Larson paused in filling his tumbler. He looked around at Brocius, clearly puzzled. The burly foreman shook his head. "It was the young one, Joe Phoebe. He's the one who brought McGinnis back. We spotted him at the bottom of Moss Mesa." In a voice devoid of emotion, he told of their encounter with Phoebe.

His jaw set, the enraged rancher paced the large squares of Spanish tile he had hauled up from Coahuila. His heels clicked on the hard floor. He downed the bourbon, then splashed more in the tumbler and resumed pacing.

Finally, he stopped, glared at the empty fireplace, and then in one swift move, hurled his glass in it, shattering the tumbler into a thousand pieces. He spun on his heel. "I want Joe Phoebe, and I want him dead. As far as Old Man Mills, burn the place down."

Brocius stiffened in surprise. Such a move was drastic, too drastic.

Larson continued, explaining his reasoning, but Brocius had the feeling it was not as much for his benefit as it was the greedy rancher justifying his own actions to himself. "The girl probably got the loan, enough to pay off the mortgage, but not enough to rebuild the whole shebang. Burn it to the ground. Tonight. You hear?"

Squatting about the small fire in their camp north of Dead Apache Springs, Red Coggins turned up a bottle of whiskey and chugged down two large gulps. He dragged the grimy sleeve of his shirt over his cracked lips and passed the bottle to Charley. "I can't figure where Phoebe went. It's like he jumped off the edge of the world."

Charley grunted, took a big hit from the bottle, and tossed it back to Red. He lay back on his saddle and pulled his blanket up to his chest. "Maybe tomorrow." He fell asleep to the sound of rain pattering against the canvas fly they had rigged overhead.

Red narrowed his eyes. "If we're lucky." He took another drink, then crawled into his soogan. He was beginning to think luck had tossed him aside and headed on up the road.

* * *

The pounding in his head elbowed its way into Joe Phoebe's consciousness, parting the black curtain enveloping him. He opened his eyes, peering up at a cloudless sky. The day was strangely silent. Gingerly he moved his limbs, one at a time, surprised to find nothing broken, just bruised. He touched the side of his forehead, discovering a knot the size of a hen egg.

Clenching his teeth against the pain, he sat up and leaned against the side of the rocky cliff, closing his eyes in an effort to still the throbbing in his skull. When he opened them, he stared at his legs spread out before him.

He frowned when he saw he was wearing rain-soaked denim trousers. He looked down at his chest, surprised to see a blue denim shirt and leather vest instead of the butternut gray of a Confederate battle jacket.

His head pounded. He closed his eyes, and images of blue and gray soldiers locked in bloody, hand-to-hand combat exploded in his head.

His eyes popped open, and he stared up into a brittle blue sky as flickers of the lost years of his life came flashing back. His memory was returning.

The image of a youngster sitting on a horse in front of a bank materialized in his brain. He struggled to put a name to the boy on the pony.

He grimaced as the throbbing in his head started anew, reminding him of the job facing him. There was no time to waste dredging up the past. He looked at the winding creek almost two hundred feet below. Above, the rim of the mesa was just beyond his reach, but two scrubby cedars, one above the other, were growing from a zigzag fissure that led to the rim.

One of the scrubby cedars had a snapped trunk. Drawing a deep breath, Joe closed his eyes and leaned back against the cool rock. He vaguely remembered his fall.

Drawing a deep breath, he struggled to his feet, holding to the lower cedar to steady himself while he swept the cobwebs from his addled brain.

Cocking his head, he examined the fissure in which the cedar grew. Using the two stunted trees as handholds, he figured he could pull himself up so he could jam his fingers into the space above the trees. From there it was only a couple of feet to the rim.

Despite the pounding headache, he was now thinking clearly. He quickly removed his boots, tossed them up over the rim, and then reached for the cedar. With his toes digging into the minute cracks in the granite, he pulled himself up so he could place one knee on the unbroken cedar and grab the second one.

He released one hand, jabbed his fingers into the split in the granite above the upper cedar, and pulled himself up until he could balance one foot on the spindly trunk.

He felt the root beneath his foot begin ripping from the fissure. In desperation, he threw one hand over his head, clawing his fingers into the rim. Without hesitation, he swung his other hand up and grabbed a small sage on the rim. With a grunt, he hoisted himself over the edge and rolled onto his back, gasping for air and staring into the cloudless sky above.

In the few seconds it took to find and slip into his boots, Joe remembered his last battle against the Federals somewhere in Virginia. He had gagged at the blood and gore, but he had no time to still the nausea, for the Union forces had overrun the Confederate fortifications. He had fought for his life.

And then a blinding ball of fire exploded in his head.

Next thing he knew, he was in a hospital.

And then Ira took him under his wing.

Joe glanced around the mesa, then pushed to his feet. Pausing to pick up his muddy hat, he headed down the trail after his stallion.

Upon awakening that morning, Charley Lasater spotted a saddled horse grazing nearby. He stared at it, puzzled. He knew he had seen the animal before, but where? Then he remembered. Excited, he called Red and pointed to the black. "That's Billy Reno's horse. That was the horse he was riding when I spotted him at the mercantile in Abbottville."

The stallion refused to permit either of the range bums to draw near. When Lasater's pony scented the stallion, she whinnied. The black horse lifted his head, then, docile as a tiny kitten, trotted over to where the two horses were picketed. The rain had washed away all signs, so there was no possibility of backtracking. Breaking camp, the two owlhoots, leading the stallion with a stout rope, started up the Waco road in the direction of the Abbottville Cutoff.

Chapter Seventeen

Before Red and Charley reached the Abbottville Cutoff, four Circle L rannies, led by Henry Clay Brocius, rode up. Brocius recognized the black stallion, and learning the two had found it that morning, took it from them.

Outnumbered, Red and Charley didn't argue.

Mixed-race Navajo Dave reached for the reins of the stallion, but the black horse bared its teeth and charged the wiry hardcase.

"Grab him!" Brocius shouted.

The black horse reared, pawing at the sky.

Curly deftly put a loop around the stallion's neck, jerking the enraged animal back down.

"Put another rope on him!" shouted Brocius.

Navajo Dave cursed. "Just shoot the hammerhead!"

"Do it and I'll blow your head off."

Dave put a second loop about the stallion's neck.

After a few minutes' struggle, it settled down.

Brocius eyed the heavily muscled animal. His eyes

narrowed. "Curly, you and Dave take this one back to the ranch. I'm going to enjoy breaking him down."

After the two rode away, with the horse squealing and fighting the ropes, Brocius turned to Red and Charley. "And you two, I ever see you around here again, you'll be looking up at daisies. Understand?"

The two nodded jerkily.

After descending the mesa, Joe headed for Abbottville since it was closer than Dead Apache Springs. There he would pick up another pony. He knew there was the possibility of being recognized, but it was a chance he had to take.

Just before noon, he came upon the Abbottville-Rey's Fort Road. He guessed he was perhaps a mile from Abbottville. As he plodded along, he heard voices approaching. He ducked into the thick foliage of catbrier and spicebush along the side of the winding road.

Minutes later, Navajo Dave and Curly, leading the stallion, rode into view. Joe grimaced. He eased farther back in the underbrush, planning on letting them pass.

But the black horse had other ideas.

Just as they grew even with Joe, the stallion jerked back on the ropes, almost yanking Curly from his saddle. "What the . . ."

Navajo Dave saw the stallion staring into the underbrush. "Something's in there," he muttered. "Something spooked the animal. Take a look."

Growling under his breath, Joe waited, hoping the two rannies would ride on.

"Not me," Curly replied. "You look. I ain't going to walk into no bear or mountain lion."

The wiry Navajo snorted and dismounted.

Having no choice, Joe stepped from the underbrush, the muzzle of his Paterson centered on Dave's chest. "Hold it right there, boys. Either one moves, and he'll end up trying to digest a lead plum."

From his saddle, Curly exclaimed, "You're Joe Phoebe."

The lean cowpoke barked, "And you're a dead man if you don't get down by your partner. Now!"

Curly hesitated, but when he saw the cold determination in Phoebe's eyes, he hurriedly climbed out of the saddle.

"Now both of you, hit the ground. On your belly. Arms out in front of you."

When the two lay down, Joe shucked their six-guns and tossed them into the forest. Swinging onto the black stallion, he grabbed the reins of the outlaws' horses. "You can pick them up in town at the mercantile," Joe said.

Realizing Phoebe wasn't going to kill him, Navajo Dave grew braver. He snarled, "If you're smart, cowboy, you'll light a shuck out of the country, or you'll get what the old man at the freight office got."

Joe's blood ran cold. He wheeled the black around and reined up beside the prostrate outlaw. "What happened to him?"

Navajo Dave grunted. "Go to blazes!"

Joe placed a slug between Dave's outstretched thumb and finger. The outlaw screamed.

"Next one takes a finger off."

The Navajo blubbered. "All right, all right, don't shoot. They burnt the place down."

Joe blinked, thinking he had misunderstood the prone owlhoot. "They did what?"

Keeping his face buried in the dirt, Navajo Dave shouted, "Brocius! Larson ordered him to burn the place."

A curtain of red passed in front of Joe's eyes. He suppressed his rage. "I was going to leave your horses in Abbottville, but forget it. I ought to blow a hole in both your worthless carcasses, but I won't. Get out of the country. Next time I run across either one of you jaspers, I'm shooting first." For several long moments, he glared down at the trembling outlaws, resisting the almost-overpowering urge to rid the world of two more pieces of scum. Finally, he wheeled his pony about and raced northward to the Waco road, planning on holing up in the Bittersweets until night, then riding into Dead Apache Springs.

At the cutoff, he shivered when he spotted several rattlers basking in the heat of the sun on the black rock of Rattlesnake Hill. He saw a seven-foot-long rattler slither down into a hole behind a small boulder beneath an ancient cedar. It was the only tree near the hill. From the cutoff, he headed up into the limestone crags of the Bittersweets.

Later that day, he spotted Ira and Ellen on the road below. He hurried down to intercept them, deciding to hold off telling Ira his memory was returning until the two of them were alone. He didn't cotton to the idea of Ellen Mills knowing he had once been party to a bank holdup, even though his brother had told him they were simply conducting business inside.

Ten minutes later, he caught up with Ira and Ellen, and together, the three of them headed back to Dead Apache Springs.

Ellen beamed with excitement. "We have the loan!"

she shouted. "We have the loan. The banker was out of town, so we had to wait an extra day, but we have it."

Her enthusiasm vanished into a flood of tears when Joe repeated Navajo Dave's story about the fire. "I don't know how bad it was. Right now, we need to get on down and see what we can do to help your dad."

Just before they reached the artesian spring flowing from the granite uplift east of town, Joe reined up. "Best you go on in without me. I'll swing around behind the corrals until after dark."

Staying out of sight deep in the forest, the rawhide tough cowboy came in from the rear of the freight and livery barn just before sundown. He reined up in shock when he saw the empty corrals and smoke still drifting up from the charred remains of the barn.

Through the thick understory vegetation, Joe looked on as Ira and Ellen spoke with the sheriff's deputy, Rufus Bird, in front of the charred building. A smug sneer on his face, Deputy Chester Rennig watched from the porch in front of the jail. The young woman stiffened, then her legs grew weak. Ira grabbed her before she sagged to the muddy street. With the deputy's help, Ira helped Ellen into the sheriff's office.

Joe grimaced. A sick feeling began to grow in his stomach. Whatever had taken place, it had to be more than a burned barn for the tough young woman to react as she did.

Backing away, Joe circled the small village, coming in near the rear of the sheriff's office. He watched as Ira, with his arm supporting Ellen, helped her along the boardwalk to the doctor's office next door to the jail.

Slipping through the thick growth of wild azalea and huckleberry, Joe made his way toward the doctor's office, a board and batten two-story at the end of the street. As he drew near, he spotted a crouching figure in a thick growth of cedar near the side window.

Joe darted behind an ancient oak, his dark eyes studying the jasper. Then he recognized the kneeling owlhoot as Curly Franklin, the same jasper he had drawn down on that morning. Curly raised his six-gun.

Joe stepped from behind the oak. "Remember what I told you this morning, Curly?"

Instantly, the killer spun and fired. His slug tugged at Joe's vest just as Joe, cold-eyed and cool, snapped off two shots.

Curly staggered back around as the first slug slammed into his chest and the second ripped through his neck, severing the carotid.

Joe remained beside the oak, watching the prone killer.

He heard someone running on the boardwalk.

Eyes narrowing, he stepped back behind the oak just as Deputy Rennig rounded the corner.

In the next breath, Ira came around the corner followed by Doc Adams, a middle-aged sawbones with thin jowls. Ira called out, "What's going on, Deputy?"

Rennig stared down at Curly, then scanned the forest about him. "No idea. You see anybody running away from here?"

Shaking his head of gray hair, Ira grunted. "Nope."

Adams quickly knelt by the prone owlhoot. "This one's gone."

"I shot him, Deputy," Joe said, stepping from behind the oak and leveling the muzzle of his Paterson on the deputy's belly. "He was aiming to bushwhack someone in the doctor's office."

Rennig glanced at the window, then at Curly's fingers still wrapped around the butt of a six-gun. He extended his hand. "Well, if what you say's true, we won't have no problems then. Now, give me your gun."

Doc Adams rose, staring at Joe.

One side of Joe's lips ticked up. "Sorry. I'll give it to the sheriff."

The deputy stiffened.

"The sheriff's dead, Joe," said Ira. "Lem too. Colley's in the doc's office, shot up right bad. Miss Ellen's in there with him. I was talking to Doc here in the next room."

Joe glared at the deputy. "What happened to Lem?"

Rennig stared at the ground.

Ira shot the deputy an accusing look. "Burnt up in the fire. That's what they told us."

"That's right," the doctor said.

Joe flexed his fingers about the grip of the Paterson. "Is that right?"

Deputy Rennig grunted. "Yeah. He couldn't get out in that wheelchair. We found Colley on the ground outside."

"You catch anybody?"

He shook his head. "The sheriff was the first there. They was all wearing masks, and they shot him down. By the time I got there, they was all gone."

Joe narrowed his eyes and clenched his teeth. "It was on the orders of Hammond Larson. Navajo Dave confessed that to me this morning. Brocius and his boys . . ." He indicated the body on the ground. "And this one too, burned the freight barn."

Doc Adams cursed. "That don't surprise me one bit. I

kept telling the sheriff to do something about Larson, but old Jess just kept whistling in the wind."

Ira stepped around in front of the deputy. "What are you going to do about it, Deputy?"

Rennig gulped, his Adam's apple bobbing up and down. "I—I can't do nothing without proof. And all I got is what Phoebe here says. There ain't nothing to back him up."

Suppressing the rage boiling in his veins, Joe retorted, "Blast it all, he's right, Ira! What about Colley? Can he be moved?"

"No." Doc Adams shook his head. "He's full of holes. He might not make it through the night."

Joe thought for a few seconds. "All right, Ira. You stay the night with Ellen. Keep her in the doc's office." He turned to the deputy. "I don't know whose side you're on, but if anything happens to that girl, I promise you'll never see the next sunrise."

Chapter Eighteen

Deputy Rennig scurried back to the jail. Joe looked at the doctor, then Ira. "You say you and the doctor were in another room?"

Ira cut his eyes toward the retreating back of the deputy. "Yeah. He was telling me how bad the younker was shot up."

"So it had to be Ellen or the boy that Curly was after. Probably Ellen, and you can figure Brocius made sure Lem couldn't get out of that office."

Doc Adams clucked his tongue. "From the first time I met Hammond Larson, I knew he was trouble. Too slick looking."

Pressing his thin lips together in anger, Ira growled, "Reckon you're right on the money there, Doc." He looked at Joe. "So, what you got in mind?"

Joe pursed his lips. "We got to outthink those fellers—" He paused and with a faint grin, added, "Like the Federal boys did us up at Phoebe Pond."

The implication of Joe's words hit Ira. His eyes grew wide. "Phoebe Pond? But—"

Joe's smile grew broader.

The old man clucked his tongue. "Well, I'll be hornswoggled. You mean you got your memory back?"

Confused by the sudden turn the conversation had taken, Doc Adams looked from one to the other.

"Not all. I'll tell you all about it later. Right now, we got to get Ellen and Colley out of Dead Apache Springs. Larson wants the whole family dead."

"But the boy, he can't be moved." Ira's craggy face wrinkled in concern.

Joe turned to the doctor. "All right, then, Doc, you get out the word that the boy's dying, that it's only a matter of hours. Let Rennig know first. I got a feeling Brocius will find out right away."

Anger flushed Doc Adams' face. "You blasted well right I will. And you don't worry about the boy. Anybody comes for him, they'll have to go through a twelve-gauge greener loaded with nails."

Joe winked at the doc. "Doc, you and me could get to be good friends." He turned to Ira and grew serious. "Let's get Ellen and light a shuck out of town. I know where we can fort up."

"But," Ira said, frowning, "I thought you wanted me to spend the night here with her?"

Gesturing in the direction Rennig had disappeared, Joe explained, "I said that for the deputy's benefit. I don't trust him."

Doc Adams snorted. "I don't blame you, son."

"If I'm not mistaken, Rennig is rounding up a posse

now to grab me. I'll lead them back west. You and Ellen head in the other direction. I'll meet you at the Abbott-ville Cutoff."

"Don't worry, partner," Ira drawled. "We'll be waiting. Just you look out for yourself, you hear?"

Joe spoke to the doctor. "Keep an eye out in the morning, Doc. I'd wager a month's pay Brocius and his boys will be here with the sun."

Ellen refused to leave her brother.

Ira pleaded with her. "You got to believe me, Miss Ellen. Joe's idea is the best chance we have to keep you and the younker alive."

She stared up at him defiantly. "Where is Joe then? Why doesn't he tell me himself?"

Doc Adams laid his hand on her arm. "Because right now, Deputy Rennig is probably rounding up a posse to run Joe down. He's going to lead them west of town while you and Ira head east."

Ellen studied the old doctor. He smiled gently.

The pounding of horses raced past the doctor's office. "There they go now," he said.

As soon as the sounds of the posse faded away down the road to Baineye Creek, Ira turned to the young woman. "It's time."

Pausing to touch her lips to her unconscious brother's pale cheek, she said a soft prayer. "Please dear Lord, let him live."

Minutes later they were on the east road.

An hour out of Dead Apache Springs, Ira reined up. "What's wrong?" Ellen asked in alarm.

"Listen." Behind them came the faint thud of hoof-beats. "Someone's coming. Fast. Follow me."

He led her off the road and back into a thick growth of wild azalea, where they had a clear view of the road. The waning moon directly overhead lit the winding trace.

A few minutes later, a black horse rounded a bend in the road and burst from the shadows into the moonlight. "It's Joe," he announced. Placing a thumb and index finger against his bottom teeth, he gave out a shrill whistle.

Joe pulled the galloping stallion to a sliding halt and wheeled about as Ira and Ellen emerged from the shadows of the thicket. "You two all right?"

"As rain, partner. That was fast. I didn't expect you for another couple hours."

He removed his hat and ran his fingers through his short hair. The moonlight lit his face. "I led them out a few miles, then pulled off while they hightailed it past me. I figure they probably made another few miles before they figured out they was chasing night crickets and fireflies." He reined about. "Let's go. We got to get away from here."

A few miles farther, he cut off the road and headed into the forbidding crags of the Bittersweet Mountains.

Ellen had passed the rugged range of granite and limestone numerous times, but had never ventured into it. No one had, for it was spoken of as a dark, forbidding realm into which those who ventured never returned.

Wending his way deeper and deeper into the ominous Bittersweets, Joe guided them to a rampart from which they could gaze in all four directions upon the surrounding countryside, itself cast in eerie relief by the waning moon.

Their refuge was snug, the large chamber protected

from the weather. There were two adjacent chambers, one that opened into a rock-rimmed basin with enough graze for their horses to last a week. Nearby a tiny stream of water rose from the rocks, filling a small pool and then bubbling on down to the Leon River miles away.

From her saddle, Ellen looked about the camp in surprise. "I had no idea this was here."

Joe dismounted. "It'll serve its purpose until I'm finished."

"Finished? With what?"

Without answering her question, he took the reins of Ellen's horse so she could dismount. "Let's get a fire going, and we'll talk about it. I have some supplies inside that I picked up in Abbottville."

After supper, they sat around the fire drinking thick coffee. Ellen asked, "So, what do you have in mind?"

Staring at her over the rim of his steaming cup of coffee, he cleared his throat. "Larson has to be stopped. There's only one way now that the sheriff is dead." He hesitated. "Larson understands one thing, power. With Brocius and his bunch, Larson has it. We got to strip him of it."

She leaned forward, the firelight casting dancing shadows on her worried face. "How?"

"I'm not sure, but I'll find a way," Joe said. "That's why I want you to stay here with Ira."

"Do you really believe they would kill me?"

"What do you think Curly was doing outside the doctor's window?"

The young woman leaned back against the wall of the chamber. She grew pensive, but her eyes never left Joe's. "It doesn't make sense. What could I do to hurt them?"

Joe grimaced. "Nothing."

Ira spoke up. "All right. Now, what happened to you? How'd you get your memory back?"

Ellen leaned forward, surprised. "Is that right? Do you remember now?"

"Some. Not all." He touched the knot on the side of his forehead. "This helped me remember." He quickly related the details of the chase and his fall.

"So how much do you remember?" Ellen asked with a tentative smile.

"Not much. But," he added, "it'll come back."

In a wary voice, Ira spoke up. "Do you remember Abbottville?"

"I do remember the bank in Abbottville. Back before the war. And I was holding the horses." He paused, trying to rearrange the blurring thoughts tumbling about in the recesses of his memory. Slowly, hazy images took on a more defined substance, like a herd of cattle materializing through the fading morning fog. "I remember three or four men running out of the bank. Shots were coming from every direction. I didn't know what was happening."

Ellen looked at Ira, confused.

Joe pulled out his bag of Bull Durham and rolled a cigarette. He slowly peeled layer after layer of darkness from his memory. "My brother, Frank, had bought me from the Apaches. I don't remember where. I don't know how I ended up with them. He rode with three partners." He shook his head. "I can't remember their names. When we rode into Abbottville, Frank told me to hold the horses while they took care of some business inside. Next thing I knew, people started shooting and running out of the bank." His brow crumpled in pain.

"What is it, Joe? Something wrong?"

Joe stared at the ground. Slowly, he lifted his gaze. "No. No. I remember that Frank and one of the others got shot. Next thing I knew, I was racing out of town by myself. Then another gang member caught up with me—the leader—but I don't remember his name."

"What happened then?"

Struggling to fill the holes in his past, Joe shook his head. "Seems like he was shot up bad. We stopped at a creek or something." His face wrinkled in concentration. "I can't remember where, but I do remember a heap of rocks. Then we kept riding. He pulled off at some house, but I kept on. I wanted to get as far away as I could. Later I joined the First Texas Cavalry until it broke up in sixty-two. Then they mustered us in to other battalions until we ended up at Phoebe Pond."

"Ten years ago. Why, you were just a kid," she said. "You had nothing to do with the bank robbery." She paused, her forehead wrinkling in concentration. "I remember hearing about it. The bank's money was never recovered."

Ira cut his eyes at his partner. "You reckon it's hidden around here somewhere?"

Joe drew a deep breath. "I remember something all fuzzy-like about gold coins and rocks." He paused. "If I knew where it was, I'd give it back in a heartbeat."

With a warm smile on her lips and a gleam of affection in her eyes, Ellen leaned over and laid her hand on Joe's arm. "It'll work out. I know it will."

He smiled in return. "I hope you're right."

Ira stretched his arms over his head. "I don't know about you two, but I'm ready to hit the sack."

Chapter Nineteen

Early the next morning, Ira ambled up as the young cowboy tended his horse. He glanced over his shoulder at the adjoining chamber where Ellen was sleeping. "Reckon you feel some better this morning, knowing who you really are, huh?"

Joe blew out through his lips. "In a way. Still, there's the name, Billy Reno. An outlaw's name."

The older man pursed his lips. "Reckon I see what you mean, but still, that's just one of them neverminds. At least for the time being." He paused. "What's in store for today?"

"To get rid of Larson."

"No one gunhand can brace that whole bunch."

"Don't plan to. I'm not anxious to kill anybody." He dropped the hoof and reached for the saddle blanket. "You go turkey hunting, you take the last one so them up front don't know what's going on until it's too late." He threw his saddle on the black horse.

"Them fellers ain't turkeys, Joe."

Tightening down the cinch, the lean cowpoke pulled the stirrup from the saddle horn and swung into the saddle. "No, but that kind of jasper usually scatter like turkeys."

"Best I go with you, partner. You'll need someone watching your back."

Joe studied the older man for several moments. He couldn't remember everything about his own past, but he had the feeling he'd never had a friend like Ira Croton. "I need you here, Ira. I'll take care of business out there. You take care of business here."

The sun had just climbed over the treetops when Joe emerged from the Bittersweets and struck the Waco road. He swung around Abbottville, staying well off the road. Later, he rode on to Circle L range, looping around the ranch and pulling up in a motte of oak and cedar atop a limestone ridge overlooking the ranch from the west.

Picketing the black stallion deep in the thicket of cedar and oak, Joe found a secure spot on the rim of the ridge. Throughout the afternoon, he observed perhaps a dozen wranglers tending the chores that kept a ranch going. The walls of the main house were rock, the roof hand-split shingles. To the east sat the barn and corrals. A large flock of chickens clucked and scratched all about the buildings. Cattle grazed the pastures and drank from the stream cutting through the spread. The creek banks were about three feet high. It was an old creek.

That afternoon, a wagon pulled up and a couple of wranglers unloaded boxes and kegs into a small shed thirty or so feet from the barn. The kegs reminded him of those filled with black powder he had hauled during the war.

An idea formed in his head. He knew Brocius, Kid Pecos, and Navajo Dave would not run without a fight. But there were another eight or nine rannies down on the ranch. He decided to see just how much fight they had in them.

Meanwhile, in the main house, Hammond Larson removed his coat and unbuttoned his vest. He glared at Brocius. In a cold, hard voice, he said, "For your information, Joe Phoebe showed up last night. He shot Curly. Now, I want to know what Curly was up to. Did you tell him to go after the Mills boy and girl?"

Brocius ignored his boss' tone. "Curly did that on his own, and he got what he deserved, though I reckon if he'd pulled it off, you wouldn't have minded too much."

Momentarily angered by the burly foreman's sarcasm, Larson shot Brocius a hard look and sneered. "Reckon you're right. I wouldn't have minded it at all." The smile abruptly vanished from his square face. He jabbed a thick finger at Brocius. "But no more killing. I don't want a hair on that boy or girl's head touched. With the old man out of the way, they're finished. All we got to worry about now is Phoebe and that old man he partners with."

Brocius sneered. "Sooner or later, we'll get him."

After sunset, Joe descended the ridge and reined up on a grove of live oak half a mile from the barn. Leaving the black stallion tied to the drooping limb of a small tree, he climbed down the creek bank and followed the graveled shoreline to the ranch, using the banks to hide him from any random eyes.

When he drew close enough to the outbuildings, he

squatted on the graveled shore and leaned back up against the three-foot bank. Studying his surroundings in the moonlight, he spotted several large boulders clustered on the opposite bank. There was something familiar about them, but what?

Slowly, lights around the ranch went out. By ten, all was dark. By midnight, the waning moon had set. The only light was the bluish-silver glow cast by the thick array of stars like so many diamonds in a black bowl.

Joe eased over the creek bank, and like the scent of clover on the wind, floated through the shadows cast by the corral rails. He froze when a burst of cackling came from the chicken coop. He waited, crouched in the shadows of the barn, hardly breathing. After a few moments of silence, he hurried across the hardpan to the storage shed and slipped inside. By feel he found the boxes, opened one, and felt inside. Cartridges.

Next to the boxes, he found the kegs. Popping the bung on one, he sniffed it. He had been right. Black powder. He could recognize the acrid odor anywhere.

Grabbing a keg under either arm, Joe hurried back to his horse. As he tied the kegs to the stallion's croup, another idea hit him. With a chuckle, he untied his pony and led him to the creek. "Come on, boy. I need you closer."

After tying his horse to a shrub on the creek bank, Joe slipped back in for another keg. Removing the bung, he poured out a pile of powder in the middle of the remaining kegs, then laid a trail of powder through the open door, across the hardpan, and behind the cook shack to the creek.

At the creek bank, he touched a match to the thick trail of black powder, jumped in his saddle, and turned the stallion back east, making no effort to cover his sign in the sand and gravel shoreline of the creek, nor in the soft ground of the oak grove.

An ear-shattering explosion rocked the countryside. Satisfied, Joe guided the black stallion up the steep trail ascending the ridge.

The exploding storage shed created pandemonium as slugs whistled in every direction.

Skillet, the cook, lay behind the potbellied stove, pressing his face into the plank floor as lead plums ripped through the clapboard walls of the cook shack.

Hammond Larson jumped to his feet and peered out the window at the fire. "What the Sam Hill . . . ?" The glass in a nearby window shattered. He jerked away, pressing up against the rock walls. He cursed. "Phoebe!" he shouted. "I'll kill you for this."

Joe knew he would be tracked. That's what he counted on. He would be waiting for them. He wound his way up the ridge and waited for sunrise.

With the coming of false dawn, he surveyed his surroundings. Below the rim, the trail forked.

Thirty feet beyond the fork, Joe spotted an ideal place for his first charge, at the base of a granite upthrust leaning over the trail below. At that point, the walls of the narrow canyon were twenty feet high.

He turned onto a narrow path leading up to the rim and quickly set the keg in place.

Joe cached the second barrel in a nearby cave. As he stepped from the cave, he felt something crawling on his shoulder and looked around. It was a centipede almost six inches long. He jumped back and slapped at the scurrying creature, knocking it to the ground. Striking a match, he held it inside the cave and spotted several black and red centipedes on the rough ceiling above.

By now, false dawn had given way to sunrise. He swung into the saddle and cut across the ridge to the fork, where he found a passage down to the rim of the second trail.

Down below, the band of wranglers found his trail. They were too distant to recognize any of the riders, but Joe knew Brocius would be leading them. His eyes narrowed as the riders disappeared beneath the canopy of limbs covering the oak grove.

Riding back to the first trap, Joe shucked his Yellow Boy from its boot. From where he sat, he could see the fork in the narrow pass and the keg at the base of the granite slab.

Navajo Dave rode up beside Henry Clay Brocius. "That gent must have been in one big hurry to leave such a plain sign behind."

Brocius' eyes narrowed. The hair on the back of his neck bristled. "Maybe, maybe not." From the beginning, he had sensed that Joe Phoebe was not just the average wrangler. He wasn't sure exactly what made him believe such, but the broad-shouldered foreman wished now he had killed Joe Phoebe that night behind the saloon.

That gent was fast and deadly with a six-gun. Jimmy the Deuce was ample proof of that. And he wasn't afraid to take chances. Blowing up the storage shed right in the middle of the ranch was more than enough evidence of his daring. Brocius shook his head. "That's what I get for trying to give a man a break."

Chapter Twenty

Brocius paused at the base of the trail leading up the ridge. A tiny warning sounded in his head. The pass was a natural for ambush. A couple of years back, a band of renegade Kiowa-Apache had caught him and some of the wranglers in it.

The grass would be waving over him now if a lucky shot hadn't killed their chief. By the time the band regrouped, Brocius and his wranglers had made their escape.

He pursed his thick lips. Yep, he knew exactly what kind of danger they faced up there. He wheeled his horse about. "We're going up, boys. Keep your eyes open. There's a thousand spots up yonder that Phoebe could come out of. Don't ask no questions. If you see him, shoot!"

Ten minutes later, they reached the fork. "Navajo, you take half and go straight. The rest of you follow me," he said, taking the right fork.

From where he sat astride his black horse behind an ancient cedar, Joe watched as the group led by Navajo

Dave approached the upthrust. He wasn't anxious to kill anyone. That, if necessary, would come later. Right now, all he wanted to do was put a scare in those who were not committed to Hammond Larson. Thin the odds a mite.

When Navajo Dave approached within thirty feet of the slanted upthrust, Joe pulled the butt of his Yellow Boy into his shoulder and squeezed off a shot. With the roar of a thousand thunderstorms, the powder exploded, sending shards of rock high into the air.

Instantly, Joe wheeled about and raced for the right fork of the shallow canyon. By the time he reached it, Brocius and his boys were galloping back down the trail to where the two canyons met.

He quickly dismounted, grabbed his lariat, and swung out a loop. As the last wrangler raced past, Joe dropped the loop over his shoulders, pinning his arms to his sides, and yanked him from the saddle. Dallying the rope around the trunk of a scrub oak, Joe pulled the screaming wrangler off the ground, leaving him dangling against the granite wall of the pass.

After throwing a couple of hitches in the rope, Joe made his way down the rim to the struggling wrangler. "Stop jumping around. I ain't going to hurt you."

Trying to look up and over his shoulder, the enraged wrangler shouted, "Let me down, and I'll plow up the ground with you, whoever you are."

"Keep yelling, and I'll leave you hanging there."

The old wrangler grew silent.

"Pass word on to Larson and Brocius. Come sunup to-morrow, I start playing serious. Any old boy who doesn't want in a fight had best leave. Ride out today, I won't bother you. Stay, and I'll shoot anyone on sight. You won't be able to step out of the cook shack or run to the outhouse with-out dodging a lead bee."

By now, the anger had fled the cowboy's red face. "Cut me down. I'll ride out. Whatever is between you and Lar-son ain't none of my business. I ain't getting myself kilt for nobody except me."

Joe pulled out his knife. "What's your name?"

"Sweet. Harry Sweet." He started twisting at the ropes again.

"All right, Harry. I said stop squirming and I'd cut you down."

Harry stopped struggling. "Yes, sir, you did."

"And I mean what I said about tomorrow just as much." He leaned down and sliced the rope in two.

Harry hit the ground and fell. By the time he clam-bered to his feet and shucked his six-gun, Joe had vanished. All he could hear were hoofbeats fading away beyond the rim.

"He said what?" The enraged foreman's eyes blazed with hate when Harry Sweet relayed Joe's message.

"That's what he said, Brocius," Harry replied. "Anyone who doesn't want part of the fight had best start drifting. He said the killing starts come sunup tomorrow."

Several of the wranglers looked at each other, indecision scribed across their sun-browned faces.

"Why, that—" Brocius erupted in a string of obsceni-ties. "That jasper's got another think coming. I'll run him down and string him up from the nearest tree." He paused, hate simmering in his black eyes as he focused them on his men. As he spoke, his voice rose until it was almost shrill. "You hear me? We ain't waiting until sunup.

We're starting now. We're going to run that no-account drifter down and leave him dangling for the buzzards. And we ain't stopping 'til we get him. Every one of you understand?" His eyes were cauldrons of red-hot anger as he glared at Harry Sweet.

Sensing that Brocius was teetering on the verge of exploding into an irrational rage, the older wrangler just nodded. Harry Sweet was a seasoned cowboy, having drifted around the Southwest for the last twenty years. In those years, much of the wisdom he had gained came from making foolish mistakes, so he knew there were times to talk and times to keep your mouth closed tighter than two coats of paint.

This was one of those times to say nothing. Henry Clay Brocius had made it clear he would tolerate no one pulling stakes. *No,* the old cowhand told himself, *I'll just wait for the right time*.

Brocius shouted at Navajo Dave, "Take half the men and head up the fork back there. I'll take the other half and drop back down in the valley and swing around the ridge. Phoebe's up there on top somewhere."

"Whatever you say, boss." The Navajo spurred his pony back down the trail to the fork.

Midafternoon, Brocius reined up in a motte of cottonwoods surrounding a watering hole. Half a dozen range cows looked around as riders approached, then lazily meandered back among the trees.

Their search proved futile. Joe Phoebe had disappeared faster than an old maid crawling under the bed.

Harry had removed his hat and was wiping down his heated face with a wet neckerchief. His riding partner,

Loopy Boles, squatted beside him and wet his own necker-chief. Under his breath, Loopy spoke softly. "What do you think about all this?"

The two had partnered ever since Harry hired on. He could trust Loopy. "I don't like it. It ain't my fight."

"But it's only one man out there. One against a dozen."

"Makes me no nevermind. Something in that feller's voice told me he ain't playing games."

"So, what you got in mind?"

Harry lowered his voice to a mere whisper. "First chance I get, I'm lighting a shuck out of here."

"What about your pay? Payday's next week."

Harry chuckled. "Thirty dollars against my life? Not good enough odds, old friend."

In the middle of the afternoon, Brocius reined up his search party when he heard a distant gunshot back to the north.

Kid Pecos pulled up beside him and gestured in the direction of the gunfire. "What do you think?"

Pursing his lips, the brawny foreman slowly shook his head. "Don't know, but I reckon we'll take a look."

They found nothing.

By then, Joe Phoebe had draped the deer on the stal-lion's croup and was headed for Dead Apache Springs to check on Colley before swinging back to the Bittersweets. It had been a long day, but he reckoned he'd set a few minds a-thinking.

Just before sundown, the two search parties met and headed back to the ranch. As he drew near the ranch, Brocius' eyes narrowed when he spotted writing on the clapboard walls of the cook shack. Behind him came a puzzled murmur from the other wranglers, all curious as to the writing. When he drew close enough to read the message, Brocius exploded in a torrent of curses.

Loopy leaned toward Harry. "What do it say, Harry? You know I can't read."

Had there been any question in Harry's mind about leaving, there was none now. A chill ran down his spine when he read the words to Loopy. "It says 'leave or die.' "

Brocius screamed, "Skillet! Where in the blazes are you? Get your worthless carcass out here."

The bone-thin cook ambled up to the open door, drying his hands on a towel. He frowned. "What's the trouble, Brocius?"

The enraged foreman jabbed a finger at the message. "That's what's wrong. Who done it?"

"Done what?" Skillet drawled, stepping out onto the hardpan and peering at the wall. Slowly, he made out the words. He looked back up at the foreman. "What's it all about? Which one of you old boys done that?"

Brocius didn't answer. He gritted his teeth and hissed, "I know who done it. What I want to know is where was you when that sneaking sidewinder wrote all them words."

The puzzled old man shook his head. "I been inside there all afternoon whipping up grub for you fellers. I never saw or heard nothing, and I kept the door open all day. Whoever done it was mighty quiet." He paused and looked around nervously. "Injun quiet," the old cook added.

Harry and Loopy exchanged worried looks.

That night in the bunkhouse, the main topic of conversation was the message on the wall. Several of the wranglers expressed apprehension about the coming day, but none expressed intent to leave, not with Navajo Dave and Kid Pecos bunking in the same room.

Back in the Bittersweets, Joe leaned back against his saddle, enjoying a hot cup of six-shooter coffee and broiled venison steaks while he related the events of the last couple of days. "And," he added, smiling at Ellen, "I swung by town. Colley's holding his own, although the doc is spreading word he's just about gone."

"You took a chance on that deer, didn't you, partner?" Ira sipped his own coffee.

"They was two or three miles away. I had enough time. I could have probably dressed it out there and still got away with time to spare."

Ira hooked his thumb at the pile of entrails down the slope. "Tomorrow, I best haul them on down to the bluff and throw them in the creek."

Joe winked at Ellen. "Reckon so. They'll soon start smelling mighty rank."

The old Johnny Reb changed the subject. "You figure any of them rannies plan on leaving?"

Joe glanced at Ellen, who stared at him, fear brimming in her eyes. "I hope so. I gave them something to think about today. I'll know tomorrow."

Ellen spoke up. "What about your memory? You been able to recollect anything else?"

"Sometimes I think I've got a hold of something, and then it just sort of fades away." He paused, then added with a wry edge in his voice, "But to tell the truth, I been a mite too busy to spend time sifting back through my own thoughts." He downed the last of his coffee and lay back on the saddle. "Reckon I'll get a few winks. I got to move out before the sun."

Three hours before sunrise, Joe rode out with extra lariats he had picked up back at the mercantile in Abbott-ville. Even if none of the wranglers had pulled their pickets, today might convince some of them to change their minds. He laughed at the thought. *Yep, some of you galoots are going to be in for a mighty big surprise.*

Chapter Twenty-one

It was still dark when Joe reached the steep trail ascending Moss Mesa, the same route he had taken when he hauled the dead body of Jimmy the Deuce back to the Circle L. Working by starlight, Joe set his first trap across the narrow trail at the base of the mesa. He tied one end of a lariat several feet off the ground to a tree trunk, laid it across the trail and covered it with leaves, then looped the other end through a fork in a tree across the narrow road, tying it around a large boulder he had hoisted up on top of another.

It was the same trap the Federals had utilized against the Texas Cavalry patrols at Cainsville, Tennessee, in 1863.

The trap was a simple one. To trigger it, he just had to knock off a small boulder from a larger one as he raced past. Seeing it was too heavy to be knocked off easily, he tilted it slightly and placed a fist-size rock beneath one side. Knocking the small rock loose would be simple, and the heavy boulder would topple to the ground ten feet below, tightening the rope to strike the following riders neck high.

He stepped back and studied the trap, grinning in satisfaction. His smile faded when he remembered how two of his tent mates had been killed by such a trap.

His next one was beyond the mesa on the narrow road winding through rocky crags and over lush pastures to the ranch. At a bend in the narrow road, he set the same type of trap once again.

Now all he had to do was lure the flies to the honey.

As the sun rose over the serrated ridges to the east of the Circle L, Brocius once again split the wranglers into two groups. He led one, Navajo Dave the other.

Harry Sweet leaned toward Loopy. "Well, at least Phoebe didn't leave us a love note last night."

Loopy shook his head. "Yeah."

The two wranglers' eyes met in an unspoken agreement. Each knew exactly what the other would do at the first opportunity.

Brocius led his party west and sent Navajo Dave north.

The air was still, a portent of another blistering summer day. Dust billowed up about the horses' hooves.

Thirty minutes later, the brawny foreman cut south with Kid Pecos, Harry Sweet, and Loopy. The other three wranglers in his party he sent west along the road to the mesa.

Seeing nothing but cattle, deer, and the occasional rabbit, the three wranglers soon grew bored. An hour passed, then one stiffened in his saddle and jerked on his reins. "Look yonder. There he is. Phoebe!"

A hundred yards up the road, Joe sat in his saddle staring at them, a four-foot branch resting across his saddle horn. Instantly, the three waddies spurred their horses. Joe wheeled about and headed for the mesa, just as the Federal decoys had years earlier.

He held the reins tight, keeping the stallion in a trot as the three quickly closed on him. Just as he approached the bend, he gave the black horse his head, and the long-coupled stallion leaped forward.

As the sprinting horse shot past the first trap, Joe stood in the stirrups and swung the thick branch, knocking the trigger rock from beneath the boulder. The rope snapped taut over the road.

Without slowing his pace when he hit the bottom of the trail leading to the crest of Moss Mesa, Joe turned in his saddle in time to see the front-running hardcase swept off his pony as his horse shot beneath the tight rope. The other two wranglers managed to duck the rope and continue their pursuit.

Joe shot over the mesa and down the far side with the two waddies less than thirty yards behind. The rocks off to his left spit shards of granite as the two tried to nail him with their six-guns. Joe leaned lower in the saddle. At thirty yards on horseback, revolvers were notoriously inaccurate, but there was always that one in a million possibility.

At the base of the ridge, he rounded the bend and triggered his second trap.

He kept the stallion in a full gallop until he put another bend behind him, and then he reined the hard-breathing animal off the road into a cluster of cedar.

A sharp yelp echoed through the forest. Joe waited, but no rider appeared.

*   *   *

When Brocius heard the distant pop of gunfire off to the north, he wheeled about and raced toward it, with Kid Pecos close behind. Loopy and Sweet waited until the two had vanished into the thick forest, then headed for the Rey's Fort Road a few miles out of Abbottville. Once there, they planned to just keep on riding.

Joe made a wide swing back to the east, coming up on the ranch from the south. Picketing his black horse by a pool of sweet water in a cul-de-sac of rocks on one of the craggy ridges overlooking the ranch, he followed a shallow but brushy arroyo down to the creek running nearest Larson's spread.

Once again, his attention was drawn to the cluster of boulders. For a moment, he tried to figure out what was so familiar about them. He had the disconcerting feeling he'd seen them well before the last couple of days.

He shook his head and turned back to the ranch, peering over the creek bank, studying the deserted layout. *Reckon Larson has them all out after me,* he said to himself. Suddenly, he ducked.

The cook, Skillet, rounded the corner of the cook shack and tossed out a bucket of dishwater. As soon as the old biscuit-roller disappeared around the corner, Joe eased over the creek bank and rose into a crouch. Moving silently, he headed for the clapboard cabin.

Later, back up on the ridge, Joe made himself comfortable while he waited for the ranch hands to return.

Fists jammed in his hips, Hammond Larson glared at his foreman. "What the Sam Hill do you mean, we only got eight or ten riders left? There was a dozen this morning."

"One was kilt when he run into a trap Phoebe set. Another one busted up his arm and leg in a dozen places. Four just disappeared, and Skillet hightailed it too."

Larson's square face grew red with anger. "What do you mean, disappeared? How could they disappear?"

Brocius sneered. "They just didn't come back; that's how. The Navajo said he run into Skillet headed for the Rey's Fort Road. Skillet was scared white as milk. Said Phoebe just walked into the cook shack big as life and claimed he was coming back in the morning. If Skillet was still here, he'd shoot 'em between the eyes."

Larson let loose with another stream of curses. "Who we got left?"

Brocius shrugged. "Me, Dave, Kid Pecos, Del Rio, Posthole, and Shorty. A couple more."

Rolling his broad shoulders, Larson growled at his foreman. "We got to figure out how to bring him to us. That's the only way. We tried to run him down, and that didn't work."

"How about getting that deputy, Rennig, to put together a posse and run him down?"

Larson snorted. "Rennig ain't smart enough to find his boots in the dark. No, there's got to be another way." His eyes lit. "The girl. What's her name? Ellen? Grab her! Get her out here. Phoebe'll come for her."

Brocius grunted. "She's gone. According to that deputy, while Phoebe had him out chasing shadows, the girl and that old Johnny Reb disappeared. Nobody's seen 'em since."

"The boy. The Mills boy. He still at the doctor's?"

"If he ain't croaked. Doc said he was about ready to go anytime."

A cruel smile ticked up one edge of the rancher's lips. "Tomorrow. Get him. Bring him out here."

"What about you not wanting to hurt a hair on him or the sister's head?" There was no accusation in his tone, merely a statement of fact.

Larson glared at the foreman. "I was wrong."

"What if the boy croaks after we get him?"

"Phoebe won't know. All he'll know is that we got the boy, and he's got to come after him."

"What if he don't?"

Larson sneered. "From what I've figured out about that Joe Phoebe, he isn't the kind not to."

From his cold camp high on the craggy ridge, Joe counted only a handful of wranglers. Earlier, he had spotted Skillet riding out on his old bony mare. With a sigh of satisfaction, he knew his plan was working. Joe wasn't sure exactly what his next step was, but he'd figure out something to keep them on edge.

Pushing to his feet, he reckoned he'd ride on back to the camp up in the Bittersweets, and then a thought hit him, a recollection of the time he and his patrol tried to hide in a deserted church to avoid a Federal patrol, but the fleas were so bad, they had to scoot out. Luckily, the Federal Yankees had passed on by.

He couldn't resist a crooked smile. "Reckon there's fleas, and then there's fleas."

Rummaging through his saddlebags, he pulled out the leather pouches containing the powder for his Colt. One of the bags was almost empty, so he split the remaining powder among the other pouches.

The bag was about eight by ten inches with a drawstring at the top. He turned it inside out to shake out as much residue powder as possible. He chuckled.

Five minutes later, he was heading to the cave where he had cached the second keg of powder.

The sun was teetering on the horizon when Joe reined up in front of the cave. Dismounting, he turned up his collar, buttoned it at the neck, tugged his hat down, slipped on his leather gloves, pulled out the powder bag, and then snapped off a couple of dead sage branches and touched a match to them. A small flame began to grow.

With the open bag in one hand and the burning brand in the other, Joe entered the centipede-infested cave. A brief touch of the flame to a red and black centipede on the ceiling, and the arthropod dropped into the bag. Within minutes, Joe had close to thirty. Quickly retreating from the cave, he snugged down the mouth of the bag, noting the movement of the soft leather as the centipedes squirmed about. By the time he emerged from the cave, night had settled over the ridges and valleys. Far below, dim lights flickered on the Circle L, tiny pinpricks of yellow in a bowl of black. Joe picked his way down the ridge to the oak grove and dismounted, waiting until all of the lights were extinguished.

By nine, the lights were out. Joe snuggled back against the tree and closed his eyes. There was plenty of time.

At three o'clock, he pushed to his feet. Any sentries would be dozing by now; still, he had to move carefully.

The bunkhouse was silent as a crypt. Clouds had moved in, from time to time, casting eerie shadows across the valley as they raced overhead.

Despite being only a two-minute walk from the creek to the bunkhouse, Joe took ten minutes to cover the distance. Each time a horse whinnied, an owl hooted, a night bird cried, he froze.

As he expected, the bunkhouse windows were wide open, letting in what little steamy summer breeze that happened to drift past.

Slipping up beneath the first window, Joe opened the mouth of the bag and lofted it through the window. He heard a groan and then a soft plunk as it struck a cowpoke and bounced onto the puncheon floor.

He hurried back to his pony and, swinging into the saddle, he waited expectantly. Over an hour passed before there was any sound or movement from below.

A shout broke the silence, followed by a string of curses. "Something bit me!" one wrangler shouted. A light shone through the window and another voice screamed. "Centipedes! Centipedes!"

Shots rang out. Other frantic voices joined in, and panicking cowboys in white long johns erupted from the open door and out the windows.

A lantern flared up outside. The cowpokes milled about, and then two entered the bunkhouse. A barrage of gunfire exploded as they blasted the scurrying centipedes.

To add to the misery of the wranglers, Joe pulled his Yellow Boy and placed a dozen shots around the rannies outside the bunkhouse.

Chapter Twenty-two

The Circle L wranglers scattered like a covey of quail.

Joe booted the Yellow Boy and headed back to the Bittersweets.

Hammond Larson raged about the ranch house, smashing a whiskey glass in the fireplace, kicking chairs from his path. Brocius watched him silently, resisting the urge to smile at Joe Phoebe's audacity. Even more so now, he hated to kill the man. Still, he would. He knew without a doubt he would, but it was an act he didn't favor.

In another time, another place, another situation, the two of them, Brocius told himself, could have been good friends.

Livid with anger, the heavyset ranch owner could only sputter when he tried to talk. "Two more dead. What kind of man is he?"

"Phoebe didn't kill them, Mr. Larson. I told you. They got shot when they was all trying to kill them centipedes. That was what you might call more like an accident."

Hammond cursed again.

The cold starlight cast forbidding shadows over the narrow trails snaking through the Bittersweets. Joe rode easily, his ears taking in the natural sounds of the night. As he drew closer to camp, he picked up occasional tendrils of woodsmoke. He patted the stallion's neck. "A hot cup of coffee is going to taste mighty good."

As he rounded the last bend into camp, a guttural voice spoke from the darkness. "Been waiting for you, Billy."

Joe froze.

The flickering flames from the campfire lit the smirk on Red Coggins' face. He held a six-gun on Joe. "Didn't really expect you until tomorrow."

Joe scanned the camp, taking in Charley Lasater squatting by the fire; his own partner, Ira, sprawled on a blanket with a bloody stain on his shirt; and Ellen sitting at Ira's side and staring up at him in fear. "Are you all right, Miss Ellen?"

The slight young woman tried to smile. "Yes, but Ira's unconscious. He's hurt bad. The bullet's still in him."

Holding tight reins on his temper, Joe looked back around at Red. "What's this all about?"

"Toss that hogleg down first."

Joe did as he was told.

Red gestured with the muzzle of his six-gun for Joe to dismount. "You know what it's about. We heard in town from the doctor you got your memory back. We want the bank money. Fifty thousand that Rafe Borke and you got off with. Where is it? Tell us and we'll let these two live."

Joe's brain raced. He had no idea of the location of the bank gold. He played for time. "That was a long time ago, Red. Things around here have changed."

"Don't hand me that," the small gunman said.

"Yeah," Charley chimed in. "Don't hand us that."

The lean young man gestured to Ira. "At least let me take care of him first."

"Forget him," Charley growled.

Red interrupted. "Nah. You go ahead and fix him up, and then you're going to take us to that bank money, or we'll put this little filly in the same shape as your partner."

Ellen gasped.

Joe dismounted and quickly knelt by the old Johnny Reb. The old man was burning with fever. Joe looked around at Ellen. "When did this happen?"

"Just after dark."

"Yeah, thanks to them buzzards." Red glanced around the camp. "I got to admit, Billy, you got a snug hideout. I'd have never thought of looking up here in these wilds. When we seen them buzzards circling, we figured on eye-balling what they was after."

Joe remembered Ira saying he was going to toss the deer entrails off the bluff. He cursed himself for not dressing the animal back by the Waco road. Too late now. He spoke to Ellen. "Get me some hot water."

While the water boiled, Joe cut away Ira's shirt, revealing a black hole in the old man's side. With Ellen holding a torch, Joe deftly probed the wound for the bullet.

Ira's face contorted in pain. An anguished groan escaped his parched lips.

After two or three gentle probes, Joe located the lead ball. Working as quickly as he could, he dug it out. Finally, he sat back, taking a deep breath and blowing it out noisily. "Well, it might not be a neat job, but the slug's out." He washed the wound, poured a dollop of whiskey on it, and then, using a fresh cloth, fashioned a bandage.

Taking a deep breath, he dropped his chin to his chest and sighed. Ellen laid her hand on his arm. "He'll be fine. How about you?"

"Forget about him, lady," Red barked. "All right, Billy. You done your good deed. Now, where's the gold?" He cocked the hammer of his six-gun and aimed it at Ira. "Or do I make sure all that work you just did was for nothing?"

Joe gestured to the coffeepot. "Can I have some?"

"Sure. No, hold it." Red leered at Ellen. "You pour him a cup, missy. And no tricks."

She handed Joe a cup of thick coffee. He scooted around and sat cross-legged beside Ira. Holding the cup in both hands, he took a small drink. "Ahh," he sighed as the warm liquid slid down his throat, heating his belly. His brain raced for some way to extricate them from the trap closing about them. He looked at Red. "First off, I don't remember a whole lot. I remember the bank job. I remember Frank getting shot down, and someone else too."

"That was McCall," Red said. "And an hombre named Donovan."

"Then I rode out of town. Next thing I knew, someone was beside me. I guess it was Rafe." He paused. "After that, everything was all blurry."

Red clenched his teeth and took a step forward. He jammed the muzzle of his six-gun in Ellen's side. His voice cold and his face twisted with frustration, he said, "It better not be all that blurry, you understand me, Billy?"

Fixing his eyes on Red, Joe replied, "I understand."

"Good. Now, where is it?"

Speaking slowly and deliberately, hoping the two owl-hoots would believe he was indeed pulling his recollections from a blurry memory, he continued. "Like I said, Red, I don't remember much, but I recollect Rafe and me coming out of Abbottville and stopping where the road ran into another one. There was sort of a dark hill on one side and a small cedar in front of it." He hesitated.

"Go on. Go on."

"Seems like there was a hole beside the cedar, a rabbit hole maybe. Rafe put the money in there and rolled a small boulder over it." He paused and sighed deeply as if he were exhausted from the effort to remember. "I got no idea where that would be."

"Hey," Charley spoke up. "I know that place." He turned to Red, his voice filled with excitement. "You remember it, Red. Where the Abbottville Road runs into the Waco road, there's a dark hill on the corner of that junction. That could be it."

Ellen spoke up. "Why, that—"

Joe shot her a hard look.

She frowned, but the warning in his eyes was enough to tell her to say nothing.

Red turned to her. "That's what?"

"Why, all I was going to say was that he's right. There is a hill at that junction."

Joe relaxed.

"All right then. Let's ride." Red gestured to Ira. "Him too."

Joe protested. "He can't ride. He's hurt too bad."

Red cocked his six-gun. "He rides or stays here forever."

With Ellen's help, Joe got Ira into the saddle, then climbed on behind him to support the semiconscious old rebel. He tied his black stallion to the saddle horn.

They rode out of the Bittersweets a few minutes after sunrise just as the wind shifted to the northeast and dark clouds heavy with rain rolled in. Joe relaxed slightly. He had been concerned that some of the rattlesnakes would be sunning, but the early morning rain would keep them holed up for the most part.

Forty minutes later, they reached the Abbottville Cut-off. The rain continued to fall, puddling on the dirt roads.

Charley spurred his horse ahead. He shouted in exhil-aration, "There it is! Yonder's the cedar." The excited owlhoot leaped from his horse and splashed through the mud and water to the cedar. "And there's the rock!" he screamed, looking back at Red.

Red shouted, "Slow down, Charley, slow down!"

But the fifty thousand in gold was too much the Sirens' Song for Charley Lasater. He dropped to his knees and rolled the small boulder away, revealing a black hole. Without hesitation, the greedy outlaw jammed his arm deep inside.

Red started forward, his eyes glittering with a mixture of suspicion and anticipation.

Ellen watched Red warily as Joe held his finger to his lips and slipped a six-gun from Ira's saddlebags. He scooted off the horse and eased silently toward Red Coggins.

A terrifying shriek split the air as Charley leaped to his feet, shaking his arm wildly about his head in a frantic effort to throw off the two rattlesnakes that had sunk their fangs in his arm.

Chapter Twenty-three

Finally, Charley managed to shake both rattlers loose. They landed in the mud with a splash and instantly started slithering back to their den. Red rode up and fired at them, but both serpents curved over the rim of the hole and vanished.

The gunfire spooked the horses. The black stallion tore loose and headed east on the Waco road. Charley's horse followed. Ira fell forward on the neck of his pony, instinctively clinging to the horse's mane. At the same time, six riders came pounding up the Abbottville road.

"Brocius!" Ellen exclaimed.

Joe looked up at her, then cut his eyes toward Red, who had dismounted and was trying to help Charley.

"Get out of here, Joe," Ellen hissed. "He'll kill you."

He hesitated, but he knew she was right. In the confusion of milling horses, agonizing screams, and shouting cowboys, Joe disappeared into the underbrush, but not before assuring Ellen he would be back.

Her lips quivered. "I know you will."

Wearing a yellow poncho, Henry Clay Brocius reined up, his horse skidding in the mud. Rain streamed off his broad-brimmed hat. He stared down at Charley kneeling in the mud and clenching his arm. "What's going on here?"

Charley cried out, "Red, help me! Do something."

"Snakebite," Red explained as he cut Charley's shirtsleeve.

Brocius glowered at the wounded man lying on his horse's neck, then at the other young rider. He recognized Ellen despite the floppy hat sagging down about her ears and her soaked clothes. "Well, well, well. Look what we got here, boys. We done saved us a trip into town."

Navajo Dave rode forward and studied Ellen. He licked his lips. "Well, I'll be. The boy's sister."

The young woman's eyes flashed. "Don't you dare put your hands on me."

The brawny foreman growled to the Navajo, "Watch her." He turned back to Red. "Who the Sam Hill are you?"

Pausing in putting a tourniquet on Charley's arm, the redheaded owlhoot answered, "Red Coggins. I got—" He looked around for Joe Phoebe, but the young man had disappeared. Red paused in tying the tourniquet. He broke into a string of curses. "He's gone. Blast it, he's gone."

Charley moaned. "Red. Hurry! It's starting to hurt like sin."

"Who? What are you talking about?" Brocius demanded.

Red ignored Charley's pleas. "Billy Reno."

Brocius' brow knit in puzzlement. "Billy Reno? Who's he?"

"Calls hisself Joe Phoebe, but he's really Billy Reno

who robbed the Abbottville Bank ten years ago and hid the money around here. Fifty thousand. Help me catch him, and I'll give you ten percent of the gold."

A short laugh rolled off Brocius' thick lips. "Ten percent? How about all of it?" Before Red could move, the burly foreman shucked his six-gun and fired, sending the surprised owlhoot spinning around and sprawling in the mud, blood running down his head into his eyes.

Charley Lasater's eyes grew wide. He never heard the shot that struck him in his left temple and blew the right side of his head off.

Brocius blew at the smoke curling from the muzzle of his six-gun. "Besides, I told you jaspers to get out of the country or else."

Kid Pecos had pulled up beside Ira's gray horse. He lifted the semiconscious man's head. "Hey, boss. This here is Phoebe's sidekick."

"Reckon we did get lucky. Bring him along. Phoebe's got no choice now. He's got to come in since we got the girl and his partner."

"No!" Ellen shouted, jerking her pony around and racing down the Waco road toward Dead Apache Springs.

"Get her!"

Navajo Dave spurred his cayuse and within a hundred yards caught the fleeing woman.

Brocius gestured with the muzzle of his six-gun at the riderless horses. "Shorty, you and Del Rio round up the horses. Posthole, grab the reins of that gray."

Del Rio wheeled his pony around. "*Sí,* Señor."

The rain continued to fall.

From where he lay in the understory vegetation just a

few feet off the road, Joe watched helplessly as the mixed-race Navajo led Ellen's horse back to Brocius. Moments later, Shorty and Del Rio returned with just one horse. "This is the only one we could find, *el jefe*," Del Rio said.

With a snort, Brocius growled. "Give the rope to Post-hole. You two look for the others, then come on in when you find them."

Hunkered down in their ponchos and their hats tugged down about their ears, the two wranglers looked upon the retreating backs of the small party.

Del Rio glanced at Shorty. "Señor Shorty, I think maybe we will have much trouble." He looked around the rain-soaked forest gloomily. "Me, I not be anxious to fight this *malo* hombre who is like *el fantasma,* a ghost."

Shorty snorted. "I ain't arguing that, amigo. Me, I was just hired on to wrangle cows, not get in no shooting war."

The dark-complexioned Mexican chewed on his bottom lip and asked wryly, "You think that is why Señor Skillet, he leave?"

His eyes still fixed on the broad shoulders of Henry Clay Brocius down the road, Shorty dragged his fingers across his lips. "I reckon it is. Probably the same reason old Loopy and Sweet vamoosed." He drew a deep breath and looked around at Del Rio. "I don't know about you, amigo, but I figure on looking for them runaway horses on up around Valley Mills or Carolina. Who knows," he added. "They might be all the way up to Waco by now."

The Mexican vaquero grinned at Shorty. "*Sí.* I think I ride with you."

Joe Phoebe watched with relief as the two wranglers hit the Waco road and turned east. He flexed his fingers about the Paterson Colt he had kept close to his body to shield the powder from the inclement weather. He didn't know if it would fire or not, but now he wouldn't have the occasion to find out.

The rain continued to pour, and although it was only late morning, the day was as gloomy as dusk. Pushing to his feet, he heard a faint whinny back toward Abbottville. Moving cautiously, he pushed through the soaking wet underbrush until he spotted a sway-backed roan, recognizing it as the rattail pony Red Coggins had ridden.

The roan cut its eyes toward Joe. He froze, then in a soft voice barely above the pattering of the rain, cajoled the animal into remaining immobile as he slowly drew near.

From the intensity and direction of the driving rain, thunder, and lightning, Joe figured the storm would last for hours. That was more than enough time to do what he must, but he just hoped the weather would be distracting enough to provide him the opportunity to slip into the inner sanctum of the Circle L, unseen.

Drink in hand, Hammond Larson stood on the tiled floor with his back to the fireplace, where a small fire blazed to ward off the chill brought on by the steady rain. He looked away from Brocius as the powerfully built foreman shed his poncho and poured himself a drink.

"Like I said, Mr. Larson, the girl and Phoebe's partner is bound to bring him in." He sipped the bonded bourbon, enjoying the smooth taste warming him all the way down to his belly. Once he got his hands on the fifty thousand from the bank robbery, he'd drink nothing but the best whiskey. Maybe even some of that sissy drink called champagne.

Larson glanced at the closed bedroom door behind which Ellen and Ira had been locked. "That was good thinking, Brocius. Once we plant that hombre under the ground, then I'll have everything going my way. Old Man Madden up at the Bar M is running short of cash this year."

Brocius leered at Larson. "Reckon he's lost a mite too many head of cattle, huh?"

The heavyset rancher snorted. "I reckon so." The smile faded from his square face. "How many hands we got left?"

"Enough," Brocius said almost indifferently. "Maybe five or six. Shorty and Del Rio's running down the loose horses. They'll be along d'rec'ly."

An hour later, Brocius began to curse. His two gunnies should have returned by now. Either Phoebe waylaid them, which he didn't believe, or the two had cut out on him. "Just like them two," he muttered angrily. "Can't trust them no more than a hound in a butchershop."

Beneath a limestone overhang high on the sawtooth ridge south of the ranch house, Joe kept his eyes on the spread below while he calmly smoked a Bull Durham. He figured Ellen was unharmed, but he worried about Ira. The old butternut rebel was tough as dry rawhide, but the rugged ride could have started the wound bleeding once again. He reminded himself Ellen was with Ira. She could tend to him.

But he also reminded himself that Brocius would be waiting for him, with at least six or seven gunhands backing him up, not counting Hammond Larson. He drew a deep breath and a cold chill settled over him. Tonight, he would take lead. There was no dodging the fact. One cowhand taking on that many gunslingers, he was bound to pick up a few lead plums.

He forced the thought from his head. What he himself needed now was rest. And sleep, if he could get some.

His stomach growled. He put a hand on his lean frame, feeling only a thin layer of skin tough as buffalo hide over a muscular belly.

The rain had slackened to a steady drizzle.

In the rear of the overhang, out of sight from any eyes below, Joe built a small fire. He cleaned the Paterson, reloading it with dry powder and taking care to daub grease over the mouth of each chamber to repel as much moisture as possible.

Finally, he stretched out of the rocky ground and covered himself with his poncho. Seconds later, he fell into an exhausted slumber.

A peal of thunder and the deafening crash of nearby lightning jerked him awake. The fire was dying out. The last tiny flames flickered. He hadn't slept long, perhaps an hour. That was good.

He peered from under the overhang as jagged streaks of blazing fire lit the countryside in an eerie silver glow. Another bolt cracked nearby.

Pushing to his feet, he stretched the kinks from his weary muscles and peered down into the valley. Lights glowed from three windows at the main house. They were waiting for him. He picked up his Yellow Boy Henry.

"Time to move out."

Chapter Twenty-four

Moving quickly between flashes of lightning, Joe slipped along the flooding creek bed, crouching against the bank in the same spot he had the night he stole the kegs of black powder. Once, when a thunderous bolt ripped the black sky apart, he spotted the jumble of boulders on the far bank. A light flickered in the depths of his brain. He struggled to grasp it, but it quickly faded away.

He studied the cluster of boulders. What was it about them that nagged at him?

Another thunderbolt jerked him back to the present. He pushed his thoughts aside, peering over the rim of the creek bank. The three windows were still lit. All the other outbuildings were dark.

Between bursts of forked lightning, Joe worked his way to the rear of the bunkhouse, wanting to take no chance of a gunman hiding out.

Working his way to the corrals, he slipped into the barn and crouched in the dark, his ears tuned for the slightest sound. Blinding thunderbolts splashed flashes of light into the barn.

Other than the pounding of the rain and earsplitting cracks of lightning, the only sounds were the feeding of the horses and stomping of hooves. Joe froze when he heard the front door swing open.

A voice shouted out, "Posthole!"

From the darkness off to Joe's right, Posthole called back, "Yeah. What?"

Joe recognized the first voice as Navajo Dave's. "Seen any trace of Phoebe?"

"Nah. Nothing. Boss ought to know ain't nobody going to be out on a night like this."

"It ain't your business to argue nothing, you hear? Shorty or Del Rio ever get back?"

"Not out here, they ain't."

Shorty and Del Rio! Those were the two Brocius sent to round up the loose horses. Appears, he told himself, they opted for something different than rounding up ponies.

Now there were two gunnies less. And soon, he told himself, glancing in the direction of Posthole, there would be three less.

Ten minutes later, Joe heard the rhythmic rasping of ripsaw snoring, in and out, in and out. During the brief seconds of lightning, he pinpointed the gunslinger. Moving silently, he slipped up on the sleeping owlhoot and slammed the muzzle of his Paterson Colt against Posthole's temple.

Joe threw open one of the two large doors. Using the brilliant light cast by the deafening thunderbolts, he located a lariat and quickly bound the unconscious gunny.

Before heading for the main house, Joe checked his percussion caps, making sure they fit snugly. His powder was dry. He slipped Posthole's six-gun under his belt and tossed the bound gunman's saddle rifle out into the muddy corral.

Joe sloshed through the water standing on the hardpan to the rear of the ranch house. He looked at the back door. Figuring all the doors would be watched, he decided to try one of the windows instead.

The second window eased open. He paused, waiting for a response from inside the darkened room.

Nothing.

He lifted the window several more inches, then stuck the barrel of his Yellow Boy against the shade and pushed on it, giving the impression of someone climbing inside.

Still nothing.

Taking a deep breath, he slipped over the sill and quickly rolled over against the bed. Beyond the door, he heard muted voices.

After they died away, he cracked the door just enough to peer out. The hall was empty, the only light a dim glow at the end of it. Moving on the balls of his feet, he eased along the wall, his eyes fixed on the open doorway four or five feet distant. He could see the room was large, and the shadows cast by a fireplace flickered against the far wall.

Joe paused by the doorjamb, glancing at the string of light coming from under the closed door across the hall.

A grunt came from beyond the open door at his side. He peered around the jamb and froze. Hammond Larson was looking on as Brocius pried up a slab of tile from the floor in front of the fireplace hearth. In that instant, Joe knew why the pile of boulders at the creek seemed so familiar.

A sharp exclamation from behind spun Joe around.

A drink of whiskey in his hand, Navajo Dave stood staring at Joe in surprise. In the next split second, he dropped the glass and grabbed for his six-gun. Joe put two .44 slugs in the Navajo's chest before the killer cleared leather.

Before the sounds died away, the door across the hall jerked open. Kid Pecos froze, gaping at Joe.

Joe tossed the Yellow Boy at the killer, causing him to hesitate. He then grabbed the Kid's vest and swung him around and slammed him into the wall, momentarily stunning the gunman.

Brocius' large frame filled the door opening into the large room. Without hesitation, Joe jerked Kid Pecos around and shoved him at the brawny foreman, and in the same motion, leaped through the door from which the Kid had come.

He slammed the door and pressed up against the wall. "Joe!"

Joe spun. Ellen!

Gunshots exploded beyond the door, ripping holes through the thick wood.

Ellen screamed as a ball of lead tore a chunk from the floor in front of her. Another whining slug slammed into the corner of Ira's bed.

Joe fired back at the door, using the same angle as the

shooter outside. There came a sharp groan and a cry of pain. A body hit the floor.

All grew quiet.

Joe looked back around. Ellen stood staring in disbelief. Ira forced a weak smile. Joe hurried to the bed. "Give me a hand," he said to Ellen. Quickly the two moved the bed next to the thick rock wall by the door, out of the line of fire from the hallway.

Ellen started to speak, but Joe touched a finger to his lips and nodded to the muted voices drifting through the wall. Then they slowly faded.

Joe looked down at his partner. "How you doing?"

"Good." He wanted to say more but he didn't have the strength.

"He's doing as well as could be expected," Ellen replied, looking up at Joe.

"What about you?"

"Fine."

"They hurt you?"

"No. I can say that for them. And they let me take care of Ira here. They want you."

"You know what happens when they get me." It was a statement, not a question.

"Yes." Her eyes grew cold. "Ira told me."

Pursing his lips, Joe scanned the room, noting the door on the far wall. "Where does that go?"

"Another bedroom," Ellen said. "But it's bolted."

Moving as silently as a spider on a web, Joe checked the door, smiling with satisfaction.

Hammond Larson called out, "Phoebe. I know you hear me." He paused.

Joe crept over near the door and pressed up against the

wall out of the line of fire from the hallway. He remained silent.

Larson continued, "Let's be sensible. You think you got a lot on me, but you don't have proof, hard proof."

"No? What about the herd of Madden's up in the canyon on the other side of Valley Mills with your horses? I heard two of your boys up there, Curly and Navajo Dave."

"Proves nothing. Curly and Dave are dead. You killed them. The horses, why, the rustlers grabbed them when they drove off Madden's herd."

Joe swore under his breath. As much as he hated to admit it, Larson was right. He had no hard proof, nothing that would stand up in court.

"Tell you what, Phoebe. You and your partner get out of the country. Don't come back. I'll give the girl and her brother a job in town. Let bygones be bygones."

"You surprise me, Larson," Joe called back.

"How's that?" His words were edged with a hint of puzzlement.

"You must think we're mighty dumb to believe a bucket of hogwash like that."

Lying in bed, Ira heard a faint noise. He opened his eyes, scanning the room but seeing nothing. Then, across the room, he spotted the door slowly opening. He parted his lips, but the words wouldn't come. The door opened a crack. In the next instant, it flew open, and Henry Clay Brocius raised his six-gun.

With a Herculean effort, Ira rolled out of bed and threw himself between Brocius and Joe. "No!" He shouted just as Brocius pulled the trigger.

The impact of the slugs slammed Ira into Joe, who was spinning around. He managed to pump off two shots in half a second, both catching the brawny foreman in the chest and knocking him back against the wall before Joe collapsed under Ira's weight.

Outside the door, Larson called out, "Brocius! Did you get him? Brocius! What happened?"

Several seconds of silence elapsed while Joe hastily reloaded. Then he called out, "I'm coming for you now, Larson."

Chapter Twenty-five

After he heard the door slam, Joe peered into the hall. Kid Pecos lay dead against the wall. Navajo Dave lay a few feet away. Paterson in hand, Joe moved slowly down the hall to the dimly lit room at the end. The room was empty, but in an iron box beneath the tile were stacks of currency.

Behind him, Ellen called out, "Joe. It's Larson. He's heading for the barn."

The storm remained intense with booming thunder and jarring streaks of lightning. Water covered the hardpan.

When Joe rounded the corner of the ranch house, he saw a light coming from the barn. The light was too intense for a lantern. Larson must have set the barn on fire. He splashed through the water, and when he threw open the door, searing flames leaped several feet high.

Scanning the barn, its stalls and lofts, Joe failed to spot the rancher. Then he remembered Posthole. Quickly, he rolled the gunslinger over and sliced his bonds. "Get out," he said, turning back into the barn to search for Larson.

Two shots boomed just outside the barn doors. Joe spun and raced back. He slid to a halt in the open door as the leaping flames lit the hulking frame of Hammond Larson standing over Posthole, a smoking six-gun in his hand.

The rancher jerked his head up. Instantly, he swung the muzzle up, but Joe was already firing. The first slug punched a hole in the big rancher's breastbone, passing through and neatly exploding his spine in two. Before he could fall, another ball ripped through his right shoulder, and a third through his neck.

Back inside, Joe found Ellen kneeling by Ira, crying. She looked up at the young cowboy. The grief in her eyes told him all he needed to know.

To the east, the sun was rising. Joe laid Ira on the bed. He left the others as they lay. Joe looked down at his old partner. Fighting back the lump in his throat, he said, "I didn't get to tell the old man the news."

Her eyes red from crying, she frowned. "News?"

He looked down and smiled weakly. "I know where Rafe Borke and me hid the bank loot."

A thrilled smile leaped to her lips. "Where?"

"I'll show you while we go pick up my horse. We'll come back for Ira. The creek will be up, so you'll have to wade it."

"What difference does that make? It's pouring rain anyway. Besides, anything will be an improvement over this," she said, laughing and gesturing to her muddy denims.

Heading for the creek, Joe explained, "We came this direction after the robbery. There was no ranch here ten years ago. Rafe Borke caught up with me. We stopped at a creek. This one. I remembered something about rocks."

He stopped on the creek bank and indicated the cluster of boulders on the far shore. "Every time I saw them, I got the feeling I'd been here." He shook his head as he led her across the creek swirling about their knees. "When I saw Brocius prying up a slab of tile in the living room, I knew this was the place."

Ellen frowned. "How?"

"If I'm right," he replied, "there's a rock slab beneath that pile of boulders yonder."

Upon reaching the jumble of rocks, Joe began rolling them away. "Down here. There should be a big slab." He rolled a large boulder aside to reveal a slab of rock four feet long and two feet wide. Joe hesitated. "There it is. I dug a hole for the loot, and Rafe fit the slab over it. Then we placed some of the boulders from the creek on top."

Ellen felt a twinge of excitement, but all Joe felt was the relief that soon it would all be over.

"Borke wrapped the saddlebags in oilcloth against the water," he groaned as he struggled to lift the slab. The damp ground held it tightly, but slowly the sucking mud gave way, and Joe pushed the slab over.

Ellen gasped.

Fungus and mildew covered the bundle. Unfolding the oilcloth, Joe found the saddlebags. Gingerly, he picked them up and dumped out two large canvas bags bulging with gold coin on the oilcloth.

Before either of them could say a word, a guttural voice stunned them. "I'll take that."

When Joe looked around, he saw the sneering face of Red Coggins. Ellen gasped. "You? But Brocius—"

He sneered. "Shot me." He touched the bloody lump on his forehead. "He didn't do much of a job of it." His face turned hard. He gestured with the muzzle of his six-gun. "Now, the money. Give it to me."

Joe reached down, but Red stopped him. "Not you. You stand there. Get your hands up high." Red glanced at Ellen. "You. Lady, you get them bags for me."

Ellen looked at Joe. He said, "Do what he says. Bend down and get the bags." He cut his eyes briefly in the direction of Posthole's six-gun he had slid under his belt.

Her eyes flickered to the gun. She swallowed hard. "All right." Stepping in front of Joe, she bent over and picked up the two packages. She rose, facing Joe.

"Hurry up," demanded Red.

"I'm coming, I'm coming," she said, slipping the six-gun from under Joe's belt and turning to face the leering gunman. She fired twice.

Red stared in stunned disbelief. His face twisted in agony, and he hit the ground on his belly. He groaned, hunched his back until he was almost on his hands and knees, then collapsed.

Ellen couldn't move. She started trembling, and the six-gun fell from her hand. She broke into sobs.

Joe took her in his arms to soothe her. "He gave you no choice," he whispered. "He would have killed us right certain."

Between sobs, she managed to reply, "I know."

Chapter Twenty-six

Later that day, they reined up at the sheriff's office in Abbottville. Several curious citizens paused to stare at Ira's canvas-covered body draped over his saddle. The sheriff came out on the boardwalk and stared at Ira. He then nodded to Ellen. "Miss Mills. Sorry to hear about your pa."

"Thank you, Sheriff."

He arched an eyebrow and glanced at Ira. "Trouble?"

"That's what I came in to tell you about, Sheriff," said Joe.

"Come on in."

Inside, Sheriff Tate indicated two chairs. "So, what's the trouble?"

Draping the saddlebags over his knees, Joe related all that had taken place the last few weeks, but mentioning nothing of the bank money. "And then after it was all over, we looked under the tile Brocius was prying up in front of the fireplace and found a heap of money. It's still there." He paused. "Now, I know I don't have any hard proof of what Larson ordered those sidewinders to do, but Miss Ellen can back up what I've said."

With a laugh, Sheriff Tate rocked forward and leaned his elbows on the desk. "Things sure do work in mysterious ways, Mr. Phoebe. You believe that?"

Before Joe could answer, the door opened and Deputy Rennig from Dead Apache Springs jerked to a halt. He stared in disbelief at Joe. "You!" He cut his eyes to the sheriff. "This is the no-account I been looking for, Sheriff. The one I told you about. Arrest him."

Tate smiled and pulled his six-gun. "Oh, I'm going to arrest somebody, Deputy, but it ain't going to be that young man. I'm putting you under arrest."

Rennig's face froze in shock. He stammered for words. "Me? But, but—"

"I got me two old boys back there with the handles of Del Rio and Shorty who was caught trying to sell stolen cows. And in all the names they was real eager to mention, yours was one of them. They're willing to swear you was one of them culprits what burned Miss Mills' warehouse and barn." He gave Joe a wide smile. "See what I mean by mysterious ways, young man?" He turned back to Rennig, and his face grew hard. "Now shuck that six-gun and get back there."

When the sheriff returned, Joe told him of the bank robbery, and then turned over the stolen money. Tate lay the bags on the desk. "You say your name is Reno? Bill Reno?"

"Yep."

"And your brother was Frank?"

"Yep."

"Well, we shot down three of them. One died right off, but the other two, your brother was one, hung on for a few minutes. I forget the name of the other bank robber, but they both said you was wet behind the ears. You reckoned they was going in to take care of legitimate business. Is that right?"

"Yes, sir, it is."

Tate patted the bags. "Well, Mr. Phoebe, or Mr. Reno. I can't see where you were part of that robbery. In fact, the bank might decide to give you a reward for returning the money."

Joe grinned at Ellen and laid his hand on hers. "No reward, Sheriff. And the name is Phoebe. It kinda grows on a gent."

Ellen hesitated. "What about Rufus Bird, Sheriff? The other deputy in Dead Apache Springs. He still thinks Joe is guilty."

Tate laughed. "Don't worry. Rufus is dumb, but he's honest. I'll have one of my deputies ride back with you two and straighten him out." He paused, looked from one to the other, and asked, "What are your plans now?"

Ellen blushed. Joe grinned sappily. "I reckon we'll start the business up again, and then see what happens." He looked at her. "What do you think?"

She squeezed his hand. "I think that's a wonderful idea."